ATLAS AND THE TRAITOR

A SOUL TO FIND NOVEL

LAYLA REYNE

ABOUT THIS BOOK

I was supposed to bring balance.
That's what my name—Atlas—means.
It feels more like being torn apart.
Between good and evil, Nature and Chaos.

Always running after or from something.
Including a certain coyote shifter who wants to rip me limb
from limb.
I'd rather he shred my kilt and do other things to me.
But alas, shouldering fate keeps getting in the way.

Or maybe I've got it all wrong.
Maybe he's the only path to balance, to the future.
An end to the running.
But we'd have to trust each other first.
I'd rather tear myself apart than ever do that.

For every coyote I cursed in San Diego

PART ONE

ATLAS

ONE

Nine days.

Nine days since Atlas had rescued his brother from Vincent Cirillo, only for Cole to run right back to danger's door.

On the Rift anniversary of all days.

Atlas flicked his fingers, and a green dome of magic descended over them. It was a risk. One of the paranormals in the clearing below might notice them up here on the bluff, but Cole wasn't exactly giving him a choice.

"You shouldn't be here," Atlas urged. "Nine days is not enough time to refill your tank." If that was even possible at this point. Vincent had been bleeding his baby brother dry for years, stealing his magic and keeping him hidden. Torturing him. And torturing Atlas with the knowledge that his brother had been caught trying to rescue him and was being held right under Atlas's nose, out of reach but never out of mind.

Vincent had kept them both leashed since he couldn't catch the most powerful Shaw brother. Atlas had finally snapped his and Cole's leashes nine days ago when Vincent had pushed his own enemies too far, bringing down Nature's wrath and giving Atlas the opening he'd needed to steal Cole away, out of the back of an SUV and to a safe house.

Only to end up here, the definition of unsafe, a magically and physically weakened Cole determined to fight a giant. "I'm not letting you face him alone," his brother insisted, all heart and earnestness. The very things that had gotten him captured in the first place. He had the will to do good, more than any of the Shaws, but realizing his limits had never been Cole's strong suit.

Atlas clasped his biceps, his fingers easily circling bone and muscles, and he worried for a moment that he might break his little brother—a once laughable notion. While Cole was younger than him, he'd always been bigger in height and build. Now, he was all skin and bones in a borrowed suit that should have been two sizes too small. Atlas wanted to see him healthy and whole again, bursting at the seams of his clothes like he used to. "I just got you back," he pleaded.

Cole laid a cool, slender hand over his. "This is what we were made for, Atlas. Four brothers, four giants. You've been hunting them, alone, all these years. Let me help you now."

"Three brothers since the Rift," Atlas corrected, that day thirty years ago when Nature and Chaos had gone to war with Yerba Buena as ground zero. "And I've been hunting our other brother who's always in their orbit."

Cole's eyes sparkled from under his shaggy chestnut hair, the color so like that of their other brother who was forever lost, the warmth in Cole's muted green gaze like the comfort that used to shine from Canton's sky blue one. "You're better than that, big bro. I see you."

Did he? Was he? Were his actions over the past decade-plus altruism or selfishness? Love or guilt? Had he saved Cole for Cole's sake or to stave off his own self-imposed loneliness? It was a thin line even in his own head, a balancing act he'd failed at more times than he could count.

In any event, there was only one choice today. "I'll snap you back to the safe house." Cole was too weak to transport himself, and Atlas did not trust him to go where directed. Left to his own devises, Cole would wind up down there on that windswept stick of land, ready and unable to fight the shifters, vampires, and warlocks gathering around the makeshift altar.

Witnesses to a sacrifice that aimed to bring Chaos through the veil.

A veil that was thinning more and more each second they wasted arguing. They were running out of time. The giant—and possibly Evan, their other brother—was close. "I can get back here in time," Atlas said.

"Maybe," Cole rightly assessed. "Or I can stay here and help you. You don't have to do this alone anymore. We promised."

Atlas's chest ached, Cole's words striking at the lonely heart of him. He was so tired of being a one-man show, maneuvering and fighting solo to keep a promise he and his brothers had made countless years ago. But Cole wasn't in any kind of shape to hold up his end of that bargain.

Atlas reached again for him and caught nothing but air, the earth heaving beneath their feet and knocking them both off balance. A blinding flash of light later, and Cole was gone, using the distraction and flicker in Atlas's shield to port himself the short distance he could—to the clearing below, standing between the witnesses and the giant who'd arrived behind the altar, sacrificial human bleeding in his arms.

Atlas didn't have time for anger, fear far outpacing it. He'd just gotten his brother back; he couldn't lose him again. With a snap, he joined Cole in the clearing, his leather boots barely hitting the ground before a sizzling bolt of blue magic came hurtling his direction. Dead aim, center mass, only missing at the last second because Cole's faded green orb knocked the magic off course.

Saving him.

Atlas nodded his thanks, then threw himself into the battle that had kicked into high gear. He jousted with the shifters nipping at his kilt while Cole and the blue bolt–wielding warlock traded spells. Until an orange fireball zipped past Atlas, singeing the hair on his arm as it barreled toward the weaker target.

"Cole!" Atlas shouted. "Seasamh síos!" he ordered in their mother's tongue, infusing the words with every bit of power that ran through his veins. His brother's magic answered, dropping Cole to his knees, the giant's fireball screaming over his head and into the other warlock.

One witness down.

Atlas took out three more with the knives hidden in his leather gauntlets, then he and Cole decapitated a pair of vampires together.

"I'm going for the human!" Cole shouted. "Cover me!" He sprinted toward the altar, not giving Atlas a chance to argue, leaving him no choice but to follow fast on his heels. But before they reached the human laid atop a makeshift pile of sticks and rocks, power seared through the atmosphere and lifted the hairs on the back of Atlas's neck.

Power Atlas recognized all too well.

Evan appeared beside the giant, dressed in a tailored suit like the ones Atlas hadn't worn again since Vincent's death.

"Cole, get back!" Atlas yelled, as he slung moss-green orbs past him at their other brother, shattering Evan's yellow ones and holding him off long enough to get an arm around Cole's waist and haul him backward.

Away from danger.

He lifted a hand to snap.

Power slammed into them, yellow and awful, a split second before his thumb and middle finger met. The second after that, Cole crumpled in his arms.

TWO

Atlas tossed a handful of dirt into the open grave and murmured the blessing his mother used to recite at these things.

"Careful," came a whispered warning above him. "Someone might hear you."

He flicked the kick pleat of his cousin's seemingly demure black dress, briefly exposing the bright pink lining. "Like you being careful in this frock?"

Green eyes dancing, Daphne lowered into a crouch beside him. "Who the fuck says frock anymore?"

He flitted a hand in the air. "Old habits."

"Like you and these things," she said, fingering a fold in his kilt. "So scratchy." She covered her mouth with her other hand and raised her brows, pretending to be scandalized. "And so much leg, Mr. Shaw."

Atlas lost the battle with his laughter, drawing a disapproving glare from his father who stood nearby chatting with the parish priest and Daphne's father.

"Whoops," Daphne said, muffling her own giggle before

falling silent. When she spoke again, her voice was filled with the same warmth that reminded Atlas so much of their mothers. "I'm sorry you lost him."

He swallowed hard, staring into the distance as his mind replayed the past six weeks of hell. The gaping wound Evan's strike had left in Cole's side. The sleepless days and nights Atlas had spent by his bed, listening to the ramblings of a dying warlock whose heart wasn't ready to surrender but whose body could no longer fight. The agonizing two trips Atlas had had to make away from him, the first to dispatch a giant in La Purisima, the second to take care of another one in Yerba Buena. The endless hours he'd pretended to sit caged at Monte Corvo for the sake of intel, given and received. The crushing words Cole had spoken on Samhain, his dying wish to go home. Cole's soul had clung to his bones another agonizing three weeks, the longest of Atlas's life during which he'd been too afraid to leave again, sure Cole would be dead when he returned. He wouldn't let another brother die alone.

"Thank you for finding a reaper," Atlas said. "I know it couldn't have been easy to get someone down here." Santa Maria wasn't La Purisima, but it was close enough that the local and nearby religious fanatics made life hell for paranormals and magical beings. Unless they renounced their identity like his father had done, like Daphne's father had done too.

"It's what Cole wanted." She tossed a handful of dirt onto the casket below. Then with a tilt of her head to the grave on their other side, added, "And what your mother would've wanted." She wiped her hand on her skirt and slid her gaze to where the rest of their family stood. "Fuck what they want."

"And yet here we are," he said. "Pretending to be good little zealots. I can't believe Cole wanted to come back here."

"Are you telling me you don't want to be buried beside your mother when all is said and done?"

He raked his hands through his hair and laced his fingers behind his neck. Of course he wanted to be buried here. For as awful as life had been before he and his brothers had left, this was where his mother would wait for each of her sons on the other side of the veil, hoping they'd be delivered to her and not extinguished. Even Evan, if by some miracle he were to reject Chaos and side with Nature.

Repent was on the tip of his tongue, and he rolled his eyes at himself. Maybe he was a good little zealot after all. "We're a fucked-up bunch, you know?"

"Oh, I know." She bumped her shoulder against his. "But we're family. Hers." He didn't think she was only referring to his mother or her own. Daphne was older than him, closer in age to Canton, privy to his abject devotion to Nature. Same as their mothers'. What would Daphne think if she knew Nature was now a five-foot-nothing slip of a woman with a nose ring, bright green hair, and an attitude as fiery as her brother's red hair?

Would probably try to fuck her.

He laughed again, drawing her amused, knowing side-eye. "You heard that?" he asked, and at her nod, added, "Get out of my head."

"I can't wait to meet her," she said with a wink before standing.

Atlas shot up beside her. "Daphne, you can't tell—"

The light in her eyes hardened, revealing the battle-honed warrior her fizzy exterior hid. "I've been doing this far longer than you, cuz."

"You two aren't quarreling now, are you?"

Uncle James's question caught him off guard. He and Daphne had been so wrapped up in their own conversation that they hadn't noticed the other one winding down or their parents heading their direction.

Daphne tossed a playful smile over her shoulder. "Just reminding Atlas who's older," she told her father. "Still."

Atlas played along with her charade, bending at the waist in an exaggerated bow.

"Will you be joining us back at the house, Atlas?" His uncle's words and sympathetic smile were genuine. He was a different sort of zealot, a missionary who would rather convert the magical than banish them. Atlas's father, on the other hand, wanted nothing to do with the power that ran through their veins. Perhaps because his wife's magic had always been more powerful than his own, and beliefs aside, his father had always been, first and foremost, an asshole.

Atlas had taken enough beatings to learn his cues and to stay out of his way. Case in point, his father's expression today was as clear a *get out* as any spoken words. "Thank you," he told his uncle. "But I have somewhere I need to be."

"Your brother is dead," James said. "You need to be with family." He laid a hand on his forearm. "Come with us to church tomorrow and witness His grace."

It was all Atlas could do not to roll his eyes. Hand over his uncle's, he gave it a squeeze, then stepped back and tucked his hands in the pockets of his kilt. "I appreciate the offer, but I have to pass this time." Every time, if he could help it.

"Very well," James said, before he leaned forward and kissed his daughter's cheek. "We'll see you back at the house?"

"I'll be on my way shortly."

He nodded, wished Atlas well, then continued past them toward the cemetery exit. Atlas's father was slower to leave, giving him a disdainful up and down before turning up his nose. "Your magic won't save you."

He gestured at Cole's freshly dug grave. "Clearly."

With a disgusted huff, his father stalked off, following in James's wake.

Once they were out of earshot, Daphne bumped his shoulder again and whispered low, "Whatever hole you're going to stick your dick in tonight won't save you either."

"I'm the hole," he replied with a wink, delighting in the actual scandalized expression that raced across his cousin's face. "And at least it'll make me feel better."

THREE

Atlas hadn't exactly lied to his cousin. Sex would make him feel better. Sex with the same priest who'd officiated Cole's funeral was doubly delicious. The fact said priest also from time to time slipped him intel about Evan's whereabouts was the wicked cherry on top.

Niall's morals and nerves tangled to make him chatty, even more so if the sex was, in his mind, particularly illicit. Which was how Atlas had ended up here, in one of the private rooms of a very particular type of club on the outskirts of town, blindfolded and tied to a very different sort of cross than the one the priest usually prayed to.

"I told myself I wouldn't come back here," Niall muttered as he ran his long fingers along the edges of the leather harness that crisscrossed Atlas's bare torso.

Atlas hissed, the sensations magnified by the lack of sight. Wanting that teasing touch elsewhere, he arched his back, nudging Niall's fingers lower, over the belt that was holding open his kilt and into the crease of his groin, putting Niall on a direct path to his hardening cock.

Niall sucked in a sharp breath, and Atlas shivered. He could only imagine how high the color would be on the priest's pale cheeks. Niall wasn't an unattractive man. Mid-forties, a headful of dark brown waves, a tall, slim body he kept in shape by tending the community gardens and herding cattle at his family's ranch. And a cock he knew how to use, even if some fictional higher power made him think he shouldn't.

Niall's fingers skirted around the root of Atlas's cock. "An hour ago, I was at your father's home, witnessing His grace with your family."

Atlas angled up his face, toward the warm breath hovering close. He found the priest's stubbled chin and nibbled along it. "You witness anything else while you were there?"

"Your father was more agitated than usual." His touch drifted lower. "Then again, he's lost another son."

Atlas rolled his hips and groaned against Niall's throat. "You were barely a teenager when he lost the last one."

Niall purred as he fondled Atlas's balls. "Those were the days."

Atlas arched again, as much as his bindings would allow, body skirting the front of Niall's, heat rolling off his chest. If past experience held, the priest still had his collar on while his shirt hung open and his wet dick hung over the elastic of his briefs, his pants discarded in the corner by the door. "Were you a naughty teenager, Niall?"

His hand circled Atlas's cock. "I hadn't found my path yet."

Atlas thrust into the tight, sure grip, smearing Niall's palm and fingers with precome. "You're still naughty, aren't you?"

Niall melted into him, his lean body pressed the length of Atlas's, his fat cock digging into Atlas's hip and streaking his skin with sticky arousal.

Atlas grinned. He may have been the one tied up, but it was Niall who had surrendered. "Seems you found your path today," he rumbled low and tunneled again into Niall's fist.

"I want to help ease his pain. But with you still practicing . . ."

Atlas slammed the brakes on his surging libido. They'd somehow gotten onto him and off the path to Evan. He needed to redirect, needed to work Niall to the very edge so he would spill more of the info Atlas needed. And less of the judgment. He flicked his fingers, loosening the rope around one of his ankles enough to hitch his leg between Niall's.

Niall moaned. "Oh, fuck." Then ground down on Atlas's thigh, sliding his cotton-trapped taint and balls along the hard muscle and rutting his leaking dick against Atlas's hip. With another flick, Atlas sent a trail of magic down Niall's spine and between his ass cheeks, a virtual tongue rimming his hole the way Atlas knew he liked it.

"Oh, fuck!" Louder as the speed of Niall's strokes and ruts increased. He pressed his sweaty brow against Atlas's temple, his hot breath a heavy pant in his ear, coming unhinged with a litany of grunts and curses.

Exactly the state Atlas needed him in. He kissed up the side of Niall's face and pecked away at more of the truth. "Has my brother been practicing in these parts too?"

Evan had been a no-show in La Purisima when Atlas had slayed another giant and again at Club Sutro when the giant from the Stick had attacked Vincent's son, Paris, who'd allied himself with Nature. Atlas had killed that giant too, finally, and had made it back to the safe house in time to move Cole—and missed Evan's return to the Stick on Samhain. Evan had joined the last remaining giant in another attempt to bring Chaos through the veil, but Paris, Nature, and their team had defeated the giant and kept Chaos at bay a little longer.

And Evan had disappeared. Again.

"Not practicing," Niall said on a groan.

"But he's been here?"

"He wanted to say a prayer for your brother."

Anger caused Atlas to bite down harder than intended on Niall's ear lobe. The priest only groaned louder . . . and disclosed a nugget of useful information, finally. "He wanted me to arrange a meet at the casino."

The closest casino was located on Chumash land. The local Indigenous tribe had steadily reclaimed more and more of the southern inland territories, same as other tribes had done north and east of Yerba Buena.

Sensing Niall was close to spilling come and more intel, Atlas hitched his leg higher and rolled his hips, jostling Niall so his erection collided with his fist stroking Atlas's. Niall was powerless to resist the offered pleasure, wrapping his hand around them both, their hard cocks slippery against each other in his grip. He wound his other arm around Atlas's neck, needing more leverage and balance for his rutting, for the climax bearing down on him.

Atlas didn't have much time. He licked into the hollow behind Niall's ear. "What did he want with the Chumash?"

"Help Cole reach peace," Niall panted. "One way or another."

Niall might have believed that; the priest always wanted

to see the good in people. Atlas didn't buy it for one second. Evan was after something.

Or someone.

"Who did he want a meet with?" Atlas had a few ideas, but he needed Niall to confirm which one was right.

Instead, the priest's body tensed, practically vibrating, and with a shouted "Oh, fuck!" he erupted, soaking his fist and Atlas's cock with warm, sticky come.

And then with his next breath, he promptly panicked, his self-hatred welling up and out. "Fuck," he cursed again in a decidedly different tone. "I'm sorry, I'm sorry," the familiar litany began as he scurried off Atlas. He always did this. Every single fucking time.

Atlas was glad for the blindfold. It hid his rolling eyes as he tried to coax Niall back with a gentler tone. "Niall, it's okay," Atlas called after him, his best lead in months stumbling for the door. "You did so good. We can do more good." Sometimes the cajoling worked, but more often than not, Atlas was left hard and hanging.

Literally, this time.

The door opened and slammed shut, leaving Atlas to curse alone. To sulk in a rare moment of exhaustion, letting the cross and bindings hold him up. No one was there to see him, to take advantage of his weakness. He could indulge in a well-earned moment of self-pity. Two months, four dead giants, a second dead brother, and his last surviving brother on the run again, each passing day another one closer to Solstice and Evan's next best opportunity to bring Chaos through the veil.

And Atlas had to stop him.

Because of a promise he'd made their mother.

He leaned back his head, his world blissfully dark

beneath the blindfold, his earlier sweat and Niall's come cooling on his skin. "Did you have any idea how hard this would be?" he idly asked the keeper of his vow. "What you were asking of us? Of me?"

Times like these, he wished it had been him who'd taken Evan's hit six weeks ago—or on that day ten years ago in Talahalusi.

"But then who would champion Her cause?" his mother lilted in his head. *"Who could balance it all but you, my sweet?"*

Balance.

Sweet.

He laughed out loud, the cold, harsh sound bouncing off the cement walls. No one would ever accuse him of being sweet, and as for balanced . . . He felt more unbalanced every futile day, like he was teetering on the edge of one of those jetties in the Canyon Lands, nothing but a sheer cliff and the cold dark water below.

"It's too hard," he told her.

"There's another way. You don't have to do it alone."

Always that possibility. Always a risk he wasn't willing to take.

The door clicked open, and he stepped back from the teetering edge, pretending to be balanced once more. "Niall, I'm glad—"

The scent of dog tickled his nose.

A very particular dog.

Loathing, shame, fear, and a list of other things Atlas didn't want to name slammed into him, knocking him all the way to unbalanced for a startled second before self-preservation kicked in and he flipped over his hand, fingers poised to snap.

But that single damnable second of unsteadiness was enough for Robin to race behind him and grab his hands, holding his fingers apart. The shifter growled beside his ear. "Not so fast, you stinky bastard."

"You're one to fucking talk," Atlas spat back. "You smell like you rolled in your own shit."

"Enough," snapped a third familiar voice before the blindfold was ripped off his face. Nature stood before him in all her five-foot-nothing pissed-off glory, color high on her tan cheeks, dyed green curls piled atop her head, a new piercing in her nose. "For the record, you *both* stink." She stepped closer and shoved the blindfold between the leather straps of his harness. "But right now, you stink worse. And I want to know why."

FOUR

Atlas pointedly flicked his gaze down, then back up to Mary's hazel one. "Can I get dressed for this conversation?"

"Can you promise not to snap yourself out of here?" Robin answered, and Atlas slid his gaze to the golden one over his shoulder. The asshole coyote had the gall to laugh. "How does that even work?" he asked with a glance at Atlas's fingers still held apart by his.

Atlas scoffed. "How do you not know that?" Robin was a highly sought-after tracker. People paid handsomely for his skills—and for what the hunter did when he caught his prey. Someone you wanted found and never found again? Robin was the assassin of choice for many.

"No one's ever run from me like you do." He leaned forward, those golden eyes searing a path down Atlas's front to where his cock was still half hard. Nothing at all to do with the big, rough hands pinning his to the cross. Robin eyed him from under his long lashes, burnished gold like the rusty blond mop of shaggy hair atop his head. "Looks like you don't really want to either." His smirk was the definition of smug; Atlas wanted to punch it off his face. "I see that whole naked under the tartan thing is true."

"When I mean to have sex, yes. So, around you, never. Voluntarily."

"His snap," Mary said, interrupting their pissing contest, "creates a tear in the plane that he slips through."

"In that case," Robin said, "I am definitely not letting your hands go."

Fine, two could play at that game, especially as they were already near tied, the bulge behind Robin's fly poking Atlas's side. He shimmied his hips against the cross behind him, aiming to dislodge his kilt completely.

Mary jumped into action, covering his goods and securing the tartan around him. Removing his leverage. "If you two are done," she said with a huff, "we have three weeks until Solstice. Three weeks to find Evan."

Atlas feigned ignorance. "I have no idea what you're talking about."

"Then why can I hear your heart racing?" Robin said.

Fucking tracker. "Because I don't do *we*." *We* had gotten Cole killed, and that was just the most recent tragedy owing to that menacing two-letter word. "I don't go chasing after ghosts either."

"Then what have you been doing the past ten years?"

Atlas swiveled his gaze to the hypocrite. "You're one to talk."

Robin's deep, sinister growl would've rattled the windows if the room had any.

"Atlas," Mary chided in his head. "Don't push him."

He swung his attention back to the deity in borrowed human skin. "This again?" he mentally asked.

"It worked well for us before." When Vincent was still alive, Mary had allowed herself to be kidnapped in order to trick Vincent into hiring her to hack the location of a powerful coven. Instead, she'd hacked his network and diverted his attention. "What happened at the Stick?" she continued in his head. "I know you sent me that footage."

"I lost a brother," he told her. "I'd just gotten him back from Vincent." He flicked his gaze to Robin, then added, "I lost him the same way he lost his sister."

Mary's eyes grew wide, at least one mystery solved for her. "I'm sorry for your loss," she said. "Robin is too, even if he'll never say it."

Atlas scoffed, seriously doubting it. "He knows it wasn't me?" For the past decade, Robin had chased him, thinking he was the one who'd thrown the orb that had killed his twin sister, Deborah.

He'd been chasing the wrong Shaw twin.

"Paris saw it through the eyes of a lingering soul. He told us it wasn't you. That it was Evan." She stepped closer once more. "We can work together," she said, her aspirations for him unrealistically high. Same as his mother's. "We're after the same thing."

"I don't think we are."

She pressed her lips together, assessing. "You think you can save him."

"Not for myself," he admitted. Honestly, he'd love nothing more than to hold Evan down while Robin ripped out his throat. But for the sake of the woman waiting on the other side of the veil for him—and his brothers, all of them —he had to try.

"I promised Robin vengeance," Mary said, as if reading his thoughts. Her telepathy, unlike Daphne's, didn't go that far, but her observational skills were just as sharp. "If we get to him first, without you, I won't stop him."

"And you think *I* can?" Her answering smirk made his own hackles rise. "Always with your games. Go home, or what Canton did, what Cole gave his life for, will be all for naught."

She gasped, eyes wide once more. Another mystery solved, most of his secrets out in the open for her now. This close to the end, why bo—

A roar shattered the connection between them and spiked claws dug into his palms, making the hairs on his arms stand up.

Making his cock take notice too.

"Do not shut me out," Robin snarled.

"Take her home," Atlas bit back. He didn't believe for one second that Mary's brother, Icarus, had sent her off into the wild with their team's least reliable member.

"What planet are you on?"

"Hers." He nodded at Mary. "And I'm trying to fucking save it, but you and your lot are *constantly* in the way."

This autumn alone, Robin's brother-in-law, Adam, a cop turned vigilante, had gone head-to-head with Vincent, who he blamed for his late spouses' deaths. And while that chaos was ongoing, Vincent had offered Paris to a giant as a sacrifice. Paris had been rescued from near-death, but as a result of the spell, he'd become a medium and soulbound to detective Cormac Kelley, Adam's former cop partner and the then-reaper for the Monte Corvo ravens.

And Atlas, admittedly, had had a hand in all of it, which Robin rightfully called him on. "Except when you need us to be your fucking bait. First Icarus, then Paris. Why do you get to use us, and we can't use you?"

Problem was, they could never just be bait. If it could go sideways, it did when Robin and company were involved, which was why Atlas needed them as far away as possible at this late, delicate stage of the game. "Not how this works, dog."

The coyote flashed his pointed canines. "Oh, I beg to differ."

"Don't you have someone to go kill?"

Robin's hold on his hands faltered and something that looked an awful lot like guilt flashed through his gaze. But before Atlas could bring his thumb and middle finger together, Robin hardened his grip and every bit of the hunter—the assassin—shone in his glowing golden eyes. "Make no mistake, you're still on that list. Just in the two spot now."

"You have to fucking catch me first."

Robin's claws pierced his skin. "What was that?"

"You cheated."

For once, Mary defused the situation instead of stirring the pot. "Robin, let it go. He's not going to give us anything tonight."

But the shifter couldn't just let it go. Ever. He leaned close, nose behind Atlas's ear, his hot breath flooding the hollow there, his hotter words so low only Atlas could hear them. "I can smell you," he purred. "Not the dirty warlock stench. The real you. I know you're hard under that kilt." Atlas didn't bother to deny it. "Do you want to give me that load?"

He channeled the shiver racing up his spine into his voice, pitching it low and gravelly, hiding the edge of desire just on the other side of hate. "Not if your mouth was the last warm hole on earth."

A cold nose and chapped lips skated the outer shell of his ear. "It's a bet."

FIVE

A week passed with no more surprise visits from Mary or Robin. No more visits with Niall either, the holy man keeping his distance. Atlas had even gone to church with Daphne to try to steal two minutes alone with him, but all Atlas got for his trouble were two awkward hours with family. He was no closer to confirming who Evan had wanted to meet with among the Chumash, but with Niall's slip about the casino, and a week's worth of excavation, Atlas had a pretty good idea and was ready to make his own approach.

Dressed in a suit for the first time in over a month, he forced himself not to fidget as he surveyed the practically deserted casino. A few folks at the penny slots, a trio of guys around a corner poker table, dealers scattered among the other game tables, ready to move where a visitor might go. Not as busy as Atlas would have figured for the weekend.

Halfway through his second sweep, Atlas spotted his mark: Lucy Aguin, né Marin. According to the excavator he'd hired, Lucy was a recent transplant from the Huimen Enclave. She was also the dealer here with the newest license. Multiple angles he could work. He sidled up to the blackjack table she stood closest to.

"Good afternoon, sir," the young woman greeted, as she stepped behind the table. "You know the rules?"

He placed two chips in the box at his position. "Hit me."

A barely-there smile turned up one corner of her mouth before she righted her professional mask, perfectly neutral as she shuffled, then dealt two cards for him and two for herself. His two of hearts and three of diamonds gave him time to work. He tapped the table for another hit.

Seven of hearts, up to eleven, and Lucy wasn't over yet either.

He doubled down, another chip in the box, and tapped the table again, flashing her a smile. "You're new here."

A blush warmed her tan cheeks, but she otherwise kept her tone as neutral as her expression. "My second month."

Jack of diamonds; he was over.

Lucy wasn't, hitting twenty with the last card.

"Well played," he acknowledged, as she swept the table of cards and chips. He put another two in the box. "Are you from around here?" he asked, as she dealt another hand. He already knew she wasn't, but it was the question a stranger would ask on the way to the answer he needed.

"Talahalusi," she replied. "My husband's family is here, though. I moved down after the wedding."

"How's the tribe treating you?"

She cocked a brow. "What do you know about tribes?"

Very little, anyone would guess on first glance. He was a pale white man with blond hair and green eyes, dressed in an expensive designer suit. But looks, Atlas knew, could be deceiving. He flicked two fingers just above his chips and turned them over with a tendril of green magic. "I know we're on the same side."

She gasped, then hastily flipped over the next card, a queen that pushed them both over twenty-one. She cleared their cards in a single sweep, knocking his hand aside in the process. "Don't let them see you do that," she whispered with a flick of her gaze toward the nearest eye in the sky. "They'll throw you out if they think you're cheating."

"I wouldn't dare," he said with a wink, tapping the table for another round.

She dipped her chin, hiding her smile. "Are *you* from around here?"

"Santa Maria, originally, but I'm in Yerba Buena now."

"Ah!" she said, brightening. "I'm technically from the Huimen Enclave, but it's easier to tell folks down here that I'm from Talahalusi."

"I know the actual place," Atlas said with a smile he hoped didn't look too forced. He'd helped his former boss purchase cold-storage properties along the enclave's borders in order to hide hostages in them.

"What brings you back this way?" Lucy asked.

"My brother passed."

She paused mid-flip. "I'm sorry for your loss." Then laid down the card, pushing him over twenty-one again. She apologized again before clearing the table.

"Thank you," he said, chin lowered and swallowing hard, playing on her sympathy. He kept his gaze downcast as he put two more chips in the box. "I hear one of your elders here—Dyami, I think?—is particularly good at helping people with their grief."

"White people don't usually come to us seeking peace. You have churches and saints for that."

He lifted his gaze, meeting her dark one. "You mean big buildings built to false idols?"

"Some say that about Dyami too."

Her tone implied she was among the *some*. "You're not a fan?"

"I preferred our Miwok elders."

"How are they?" he asked, feigning curiosity. "I heard about the sinkhole and what happened to Pati Miwra." He'd engineered it in fact, kidnapping Pati for a giant Vincent had wanted to curry favor with. But as soon as Atlas had realized who she was—the tribe leader's daughter—and what she carried—a child that could end the war between Nature and Chaos, that could spare him from his role in it, eventually—he'd made sure Pati was stashed at one of those cold storage properties with her protector. Quinn had ultimately sacrificed himself for her, and in so doing, had bought Mary, Paris, and their team enough time to rescue Pati and kill the giant.

The story had apparently traveled far, Lucy's smile sneaking free again. "But Pati made it out, and her son . . ." Her smile broadened. "He's the real deal." A true eagle shifter, the first in generations. Unlike Dyami, who, by all excavated accounts, had only assumed the name. "He'll bring—"

"Peace," Atlas finished. He'd known it as soon as he'd touched Pati's arm. It had killed him to leave the very thing his mother had dedicated her life to bringing about in someone else's care, but he'd had no choice. And in the end, it had been the right call. Barely.

"It feels good to talk about it," Lucy said, drawing him out of his own half regrets.

"They're not celebrating here?"

"Not everyone believes," she said, as she swept the table once more.

He tossed his last two chips in the box. "Meaning Dyami?"

With his power and reputation threatened, Dyami would be Evan's ideal ally. Rich, power hungry, selfish, afraid. Everything his brother and Chaos preyed on.

Lucy finished dealing and glanced up, her brow furrowed and mouth open, as if she were about to agree, but then her gaze skated over his shoulder and her eyes grew wide. The next thing Atlas knew, he was being yanked off his stool by two giant men. "Didn't we tell you last week to get out of here?" one of them said.

Or maybe his brother hadn't been welcome, after all.

"Last week?" Lucy said, brows snapped together, but before Atlas could reply, the guards dragged him away from her table.

He waited until he was out of her earshot to continue the ruse he'd been dealt, angling for more information. "I just wanted another word with Dyami. I'm sure we can reach an agreement."

"The eagle has nothing left to say to you."

They hauled him to the nearest exit doors and tossed him outside. He spun to try to beg his way back inside—to talk with the man his brother had—but his vibrating phone stopped him short. He yanked the device out of his pocket and read the text from one of his sources in La Purisima. **SOS.**

The same source who, weeks back, had alerted him to

the giant there. As much as he wanted back inside that casino, Atlas couldn't ignore the text, not after the last one had proven so pivotal. He hit dial and lifted the phone to his ear.

The call connected after one ring, and Watson launched right in, not bothering with pleasantries as a crash sounded in the background. "That green-haired woman you sent me a picture of is here."

"Where, exactly?"

"The Gathering House in La Purisima."

"Are you fucking kidding me?" The Gathering House was across the street from the town's largest church, and on a Sunday afternoon, it would be packed with people eating and shopping at the local merchant booths before evening service.

"She and the dog with her are asking questions," Watson said. "The sort that will let on what they are before long."

Atlas gazed longingly at the casino, cursing Mary and Robin for making him leave the very warm lead inside. Cursing fate that wouldn't leave him the fuck alone. "I'm on my way."

SIX

Atlas ported himself into the woods at the edge of The Gathering House parking lot, keeping his sudden appearance out of sight.

Not that anyone would have noticed. Humans dressed in their Sunday best streamed out of the long, barnlike structure, running the opposite direction of Atlas, across the four-lane road toward the church on the other side. Cars slammed on brakes, some slammed into each other, but even the squeal of tires and the crunch of metal couldn't drown out the coyote's roar from inside the building.

"Fucking hell."

Atlas sprinted across the parking lot, gravel crunching under his loafers, and for once he was glad for his suit. No one gave him a second look as he fought his way inside. He hustled down the long corridor, passing merchants hastily emptying their stalls, on his way to the mess hall in the middle of the structure.

And cursed again at the sight before him.

Mary stood atop a communal dining table, wall at her

back, a knife in one hand, a ceramic mug in the other, while Robin stood on all fours in front of her, his massive jaws open as he unleashed another roar at the group of men who'd squared off against them.

"Not good," Atlas muttered.

"Not good at all." Watson scooted in beside him, as close as his duffels full of unsold baked goods allowed. "I tried to warn them, but they didn't listen."

"Trust me," Atlas said with a resigned sigh. "There's nothing you could have said that would've made them."

As if to prove his point, Mary continued to interrogate from where she stood. "We just want to know who the giant met with before he was killed. Simple question."

One of the men lunged, thrusting a chair at Robin. The coyote caught the foot rail, yanked the chair free, then flung it wide, scattering the remaining onlookers.

"Get out of here," Atlas said to Watson.

Unlike the coyote and hard-headed deity, the baker didn't need to be told twice, joining the rest of the merchants as they cleared out with their goods, only the combatants left behind.

Ten against two. Despite what the group of humans thought, the odds favored Mary and Robin. And Atlas could hasten things along. He shoved two fingers in his mouth and whistled, the high-pitched noise drawing everyone's attention. "How about we even things up a bit?" Palms up, he summoned two green orbs, and Robin yipped twice, a call that Atlas had only ever heard before in battle. And technically, that's what this was, but those yips, combined with the dancing golden eyes and stretched wide mouth, canines gleaming, registered to Atlas as laughter.

Only, he couldn't figure out who Robin was laughing at

—him or the humans? Couldn't figure out whether to throw one of his orbs at Robin for being an ass even now or if he was about to have the most fun in a fight he'd had in ages.

The quandary distracted Atlas a second too long, time enough for one of the humans to draw a gun and fire. The bullet sailed wide of Robin's head, past a fluffy ear that was already missing its point. Atlas didn't hesitate to hurl his first orb at the shooter, searing the gun from his hand and leaving him howling in pain.

"Guard her," he shouted at Robin, then advanced on the remaining humans, scattering the group with his other orb before spinning up more, chucking them each time the humans tried to reassemble or attack with whatever furniture they could use. They spouted scripture the entire time, as if it would somehow magically make the warlock and shifter disappear. Even more ridiculous were their attempts to talk Mary "out from under their spell." To try and "save" her.

Atlas laughed at the irony, a series of yips echoing him, and he had the answer to his earlier question. Laughing with him, not at him. He didn't want to like that as much as he did.

"Atlas, get down!" Mary called from her perch, as she'd done through much of the fight, directing his and Robin's maneuvers. Atlas dropped into a crouch, and the coyote vaulted over him, taking down the human who'd been coming at Atlas from behind. Robin knocked his makeshift spear free and pinned the man to the floor, letting loose a thunderous growl in his face. Atlas didn't want to like that either—or the heat it sent racing down his spine.

Thankfully, he didn't have time to get caught up in the

implications, Robin roaring an order Atlas had no trouble interpreting. He hurried to take up Robin's prior position, reaching Mary just as another of the humans had the dumb idea to engage her in a knife fight. The attacker got a slash across his chest for his idiocy, and the good little zealot act died on his next nasty breath. "You little bitch," he seethed, as he drew back an arm, preparing to lunge with his own knife again.

Atlas caught him by the elbow. "So much for that godliness," he seethed back, then flung the man into the nearest wall, knocking him unconscious. Robin flung another body on top of him, adding to the pile. But the five remaining attackers were reorganizing, one of them lighting a washcloth stuffed in a bottle of cleaning solution on fire.

Mary grabbed Atlas by the biceps. "I'll bring this place down if I have to. We'll walk out alive; they won't."

"Do *not* show yourself." Right now, she was just a nosy, green-haired human who was asking the wrong questions and in the wrong company. If she revealed who she truly was—

The doors at the opposite end of the mess hall slammed open and mangled furniture was tossed aside, revealing a hulking man dressed in all black, from his hooded trench to his leather boots to the crossbow propped on his shoulder. He tossed back the hood, revealing the scarred face of Atlas's nightmares.

"Change of plans," Atlas said and, with another whistle, called Robin back to them. For once, thank fuck, the coyote obeyed, leaping over two attackers to land between him and Mary. "Bring it down," he told the deity, then waited only long enough for her earthquake to shake the first ceiling beam loose before snapping them out of there.

SEVEN

Robin's "Who the fuck was that?" collided with Mary's "Where the fuck are we?" and all Atlas could do was hang back his head and exhale his exhaustion.

No *thank you*. No *are you okay*. Not even a second to get a drink or take a piss or to check if he was actually still in one piece. Just right into the interrogation.

"The ceiling didn't ask you a question," Robin mocked, and Atlas lowered his chin, ready to list the many reasons why he'd rather have a conversation with the pitched ceiling than either of them, but his words died a swift death, snuffed out by the man standing naked in the middle of his safe house.

Rays of afternoon sun streamed in through the structure's A-frame windows, painting Robin's freckled skin with warmth. Burnished, all of him, from the golden hairs on his muscular limbs, to the coppery strands mixed with the blond atop his head, to the swirls of red-gold hair on his chest and the wiry curls around the root of his thick cock.

Fuck, even soft it was impressive. Hard, it would be big

enough to choke Atlas, to split him in two, to fill him full and make him scream.

"Eyes up here, sugar."

Atlas snapped his gaze to the heated gold one that was unmistakably smug. Fucker. "There are extra clothes upstairs," he bit out, as he retrieved a bottle of much-needed vodka from the freezer under the stairs.

When he didn't hear Robin move, he poured himself a double, tossed back the shot, poured a second, then turned back around, marginally more fortified to face the shifter who seemed hell-bent on driving him mad.

Robin sat propped on the arm of the leather couch, arms crossed, legs spread, semi-hard cock resting against his thigh. At least he wasn't unaffected; unfortunately, he wasn't distracted either. "Now, who or what was that nightmare that walked through the door before you snapped us out of there?"

Atlas leaned against the side of the stairs. "A hunter."

"I don't know him."

"Because he only works in the South, which you usually stay out of. So why venture this way now? To La Purisima, of all places." He shifted his attention to Mary, who stood leaned against the stone wall by the double front doors. "You, especially, know better." All the trouble Icarus had gone to to keep her out of these parts, and she was right back here. "Someone could have recognized you."

"You killed a giant in LP," she said, ignoring the parts of his logic she didn't like and substituting her own. "Stood to reason Evan had been there too."

"And witnesses reported seeing a man fitting Evan's description on or about the time the giant died," Robin added.

Atlas sipped from his glass, the only thing keeping him from throwing it. "And what description was that?"

"White, short, fit, clean-cut, blond hair, dressed in a suit."

Atlas gestured at himself. "Yes, that was me, killing said giant."

Robin cocked a bushy brow, then after an up-and-down sweep of him, finally registered the change in attire since the last time he'd seen him. "What happened to the kilt?"

"I put on a suit when I need someone to think I'm Evan." The other brow rose to match, and Atlas hung back his head on another pained sigh. When he righted it, he set his sights on the biggest liar in the room. "You didn't tell him?" he said to Mary.

Robin shot off the couch. "Tell me what?"

"Atlas, don't—"

Whatever argument she was going to make was moot at this point; Robin was so close to the truth that he'd put it together any second now. No use wasting valuable time when Atlas needed answers and needed the stinky, attractive dog out of his presence. He grabbed the single framed picture off the fireplace mantel and shoved it in Robin's direction. "That's me and my brothers, including Evan."

"Brother?" He looked down at the picture, then back up at him. "He's your twin?"

"Yes, my older brother." He lowered the hammer. "By seven minutes." Robin's eyes rounded into saucers, the connection made. "Same as you and Deborah." He and Evan weren't accidentally in their lives; they never had been. Balance and a hefty dose of fate had conspired to put the four of them in this hellscape together. But that was a conversation for a different day. He needed answers, and with Mary on her heels, she was the one to press. "That couldn't have been all there was for you to risk the South."

"Someone saw him in LP last month."

Right around the time Evan would have met with Niall. "He used Cole's death as a pretense."

"Is that one of your other brothers?"

"The youngest," he said, voice rough, words scraping over the knives in his throat as he set the frame back on the mantel.

"And the last one in the picture?"

"Canton."

A low growl rumbled from deep in Robin's chest, familiar betrayal made audible.

"Yes, it's all a very tangled web." Atlas tossed back the rest of his vodka, refilled the glass, and handed it to Robin. "Welcome to the party." Unbeknownst to the coyote, he'd been a part of it his whole life, same as his late sister, same as Atlas and Evan.

Robin didn't hesitate to gulp the shot down before turning for the stairs. "I'm gonna go change so I don't rip her head off."

"Now you're catching on." Though Atlas rather liked the view of Robin from behind, his backside as firm as the front.

"Eyes over here, sugar," Mary parroted, and Atlas jutted a finger at her. "Don't you start too." He ducked into the compact kitchen under the loft and began pulling together something to eat for himself and his unexpected visitors.

Mary drifted his direction, then veered onto the couch, putting a knee to the cushions and leaning over the back to look out the window. "Where are we?"

"Safe house."

"Who owns these vineyards?"

"Me. Or, more accurately, a shell company that owns a shell company that—"

"I get it." She pushed off the couch and took the plate of cheese, nuts, and grapes he held out to her. "Hacker, remember?"

"So, tell me, then . . ." He tossed a stale baguette on the coffee table next to the cheeseboard. "What did you hack that led you home, besides Evan's maybe whereabouts?"

"Who works these vineyards?" came a question from the opposite direction, Robin loping down the stairs in a pair of sweats he'd ripped off at the knees, probably with his claws.

Atlas forced himself not to rise, in any fashion, to the bait. "The family of humans I rent it to," he said, as he grabbed a knife to cut the baguette. "They live in the main house down by the road. I keep the cottage here."

"Risky." Robin flopped onto the couch beside Mary. "They know what you are?"

"They worship her," he said with a jut of his chin toward the green-haired pixie popping grapes into her mouth. "Now, stop stalling, and tell me why you're really here."

Mary leaned forward, like she was about to answer, only to be cut off again by the fucking dog. "If we show you our cards, you show us yours."

Atlas fetched three glasses, grabbed the bottle of vodka, and lowered into the chair on the other side of Mary.

"I'm not giving you everything we know," Robin said, as Atlas filled their glasses, "so you can just run off and save your brother."

"Who says that's what I intend to do?" He slid the glass

the length of the table, vodka sloshing over the rim when Robin saved it from toppling off the edge and onto the floor. Atlas lifted his gaze, meeting Robin's intrigued gold one. "She promised you vengeance. You'll get it."

"On your terms."

Atlas lifted his glass. "Does it matter?"

EIGHT

"I knew there had to be more to the calm than just vodka."

Atlas took another puff on his joint, then glanced over his shoulder at his unwelcome visitor—who was still bare-chested despite the cool December night. "Are you allergic to shirts?"

"More like allergic to you." He approached behind Atlas's chair and plucked the joint from his fingers. "I don't trust you. I may need to shift at any moment."

"But you trust my weed?"

Robin circled the fire pit and lowered into the chair on the other side of the bistro table from Atlas. "If it's anything like your vodka, only the high-end shit for you." He took a long drag on the joint, then puffed smoke rings out of his nostrils like some kind of silly dragon. "Yep, as I expected." He handed the joint back across the table, then stretched his legs out in front of him, ankles propped on the fire pit ledge, hands folded on his abs that Atlas did not notice rippling. "I hope you weren't planning to sleep in the loft tonight. Mary's spread her shit all over the place. Never ends well."

"How long have you two been traveling together?"

"About a month."

"And Icarus hasn't come after you yet?"

Mary's brother had spent the last thirty years protecting her. That devotion, apparent even when he and Mary were simple humans, was the reason Canton had identified Mary as a vessel for Nature, why he'd infiltrated their lives to make sure the transformations happened—Mary into Nature, Icarus into her vampire protector. Why Canton had ultimately given his life for the effort, though the circumstances of his death remained a fuzzy mystery—a weighty guilt—that nagged at Atlas.

In any event, Icarus had been dutiful, staying far enough away from Mary to avoid detection but close enough to reach her in case of emergencies. Atlas had made sure Paris always had enough Daylight to sell to him for such occasions. And now, after all that effort, when Icarus was no longer a vampire but had a whole army at his back, he'd let his sister wander off . . . with Robin?

"Your pupil's doing," the coyote explained. "Paris told Mac that she's safe with me. If he'd been lying, Mac would've felt it in their soul bond. Mac told the others. That and they're probably still pissed at me for giving Paris's location to the final giant."

Atlas smiled around the joint. "He was ready."

"You raised him well."

"I didn't—"

"Did Vincent think you were Evan?"

The abrupt swerve saved Atlas from the pinch in his chest and the half-made deflection. He thanked

Robin for the small mercy with a small piece of the truth. "He wanted Evan, but only Chaos would do for my brother. So I offered Vincent the next best thing, a look-alike and the second most powerful Shaw brother."

"Is that why you don't wear the suit anymore?"

"That, and I always preferred kilts." He took another long puff on the joint before handing it back across the table.

Robin accepted it with narrowed eyes. "I can't decide whether you're good or evil."

"Do you still want to kill me?"

"Yes," he answered with zero hesitation.

Balance. "Then, does it matter?"

"I suppose not." Robin sank back in his chair, joint to his lips.

"Why haven't you killed me yet?" Atlas wondered aloud after several annoyingly comfortable minutes of silence. He expected a smirking, joking response, not Robin's well-reasoned explanation.

"Because it's apparent you hold a good many of the cards on the table. You have power and information we need in this war with Chaos."

"And when you get what you need from me?"

He mimicked a slash across his throat, added a *snick* for effect, then handed back the joint.

"You're awfully serene about it all," Atlas said.

This version of Robin was not the rabid dog he'd spent the better part of ten years running from, who just two months ago had had his muzzle around Atlas's throat, ready to end him.

"I figure, I can spend the next two weeks driving myself

crazy or driving you crazy . . ." His golden eyes danced. "Is it working yet?"

"You're an asshole."

"I know." He grinned, then stretched out further in the chair, all that muscled body burnished in the firelight.

Atlas tore his gaze away, staring at the rows of swaying vines instead. The grapes were long picked, only wilting leaves in shades of autumn left rustling in the breeze. A quiet song as one day slipped to the next. He didn't mind that Mary had commandeered the loft. Didn't mind spending time out here, sleeping out here even, after being cooped up inside with Cole for weeks, after being trapped in Vincent's compound for years. He idly wondered how Vincent's other captive was adjusting to life among the vineyards. "How is Paris, truly?"

"Alive, somehow, like Adam too, when they both weren't for a time."

Atlas shivered around the memory of Adam bleeding out on that bridge in YB. Then shivered again at what Paris must have gone through, being sacrificed by giants, twice. He was stronger than any of them had ever given him credit for.

"He's pretty remarkable," Robin said, words mirroring Atlas's thoughts. "Whether you had a hand in that or not, I wouldn't be here if not for him."

"He rescued you?"

"He gave me a purpose," he said, tone lightening, words lengthening, like maybe he wouldn't mind sleeping out here among the vines either. "Pushed the guilt aside, at least for a while."

It never truly went away. Atlas had decades on Robin in that regard. But at least the freshest guilt was somewhat assuaged. "I'm glad he's doing well. He deserved better than Vincent, better than me."

"You were him, weren't you? The way you grew up?"

Perceptive fucker. "In a lot of ways," he admitted. "My brothers and I had a mother, where Paris didn't, but our father . . . He was a different sort of man than Vincent but no less malicious."

"And yet Evan became the evil one?"

"Who says I wasn't too at one point?"

Robin lolled his head on his neck, face angled toward him, even as his eyelids drooped. "Is that how you faked it so well? It couldn't have just been the suit. Or the belief it was all for a higher good."

Atlas took a final drag of the joint, then snuffed it out in the dirt under his heel. "No, it was the guilt."

"Or your soul."

"Same difference."

Two sides of the same coin.

Like him and the coyote across the table whose body sank deeper into the chair, whose chest rose and fell with the steady, even breaths of sleep. Atlas added jealousy to his mental box labeled Robin Whelan.

He stood slowly, careful not to wake the slumbering shifter, careful not to hover too close as he paused at Robin's side, hand over his chest, basking in the heat that lapped against his palm. He was so warm, and Atlas would bet those whorls of red-gold hair on his chest were soft too, same as the copper and blond strands on his head.

He ached to find out.

He fisted his hand instead, capturing a fleeting tendril of warmth before walking away from roaring temptation and unproductive fantasy, from a fate that would only end in more guilt and misery.

He turned to the bleak reality of the here and now.

Inside, he climbed the stairs to the loft where Mary had, indeed, spread her shit out all over. She sat cross-legged in the middle of the bed, computer open on her lap, a half dozen other devices and countless cords scattered around her. "Did you get a location?" he asked her.

"I think so. Dyami has a meeting tomorrow at the bed and breakfast in downtown LP. Two of his guards are checked in there tonight."

"But not him?" he asked, and she shook her head. "Advance team," he speculated.

"Most likely, especially as a person fitting the hunter's description is staying there too."

"Do you have a list of all the registered guests?" Maybe he'd recognize an alias.

She held a tablet out to him. He got as far as the third name, then passed it back to her. "I'll leave tonight so I'm in position if Evan shows tomorrow. If he doesn't, I'll recon the meet."

"I can be packed and ready in twenty."

"You can't be there."

Red streaked across her tan cheeks, and she tossed her laptop aside, rising on her knees to protest. "You can't—"

"I can." He leaned forward and lowered his voice, just in case the coyote was feigning sleep. "Canton died for you. Cole died for you." He angled closer, voice hardened, as he threw an arm out the direction of where he'd left Robin. "He doesn't know it yet, but his sister and brother-in-law did too. Quinn and countless others. Your own brother, plus, Adam and Paris. Magic brought the latter few back to life, but it will run out at some point. You will exhaust the phoenixes. You are a temporary vessel, like all the vessels before this one, and the eagle is not ready yet for what he has to do." He waited for her to lower back to her haunches. "You have to quit putting yourself and others in jeopardy. Not as long as the deity is in there. Do you understand?"

The smile that tipped up her lips made him want to scream. "I was right about you."

He wasn't so sure. "We'll see."

NINE

Crouched behind the parapet wall of a building rooftop, Atlas took one look through his monocular into the bed and breakfast's corner café and knew things were about to go sideways. He hadn't wanted to believe what he'd read on that list Mary had handed him last night—an alias he knew all too well—but there was no denying the truth of what he saw with his own eyes.

No denying the calls, real and telepathic, that had gone unanswered overnight and this morning.

"What's your cousin doing cozied up with the pretender?"

Atlas nearly dropped his spyglass. Cursing, he spun from the unsettling sight of Daphne and Dyami cuddled together at a table to the equally unsettling shifter who'd somehow snuck up on him, not a footfall or heartbeat warning of his approach, not a whiff of dog. "How did you—"

"I'm good at my job." His gaze drifted over Atlas's shoulder. "Same as them."

Atlas followed his line of sight to the sidewalk outside the café. To the seemingly twenty-something redhead in a crocheted sweater and patchwork jeans and his silver fox partner in denim and leather approaching the cafe's glass door. Daphne and Dyami had probably noticed them already. Icarus, with his tall, chiseled frame, blue eyes, and fiery hair was one of the most striking men Atlas had ever met; add in Adam's rugged good looks and they were a formidable, distracting pair.

"They can't be here," Atlas seethed, his already sideways plan well on the way to upside down. He couldn't even lob an orb to stop them from entering. Daphne would instantly recognize his magic.

"They can be," Robin said, as he kneeled beside him. "Adam and Icarus are human. We're not."

"By that logic, my cousin and Dyami shouldn't be here either." He might not have been a true eagle shifter, but Dyami was an elder of not-insignificant influence. He had enough juice to make people think he was a shifter, by magical deception or otherwise. And speaking of power . . . "My brother definitely shouldn't be here, if he even shows."

"Except your cousin plays the convert, and Dyami the holy man."

Icarus and Adam entered the café, and Atlas hung his head, no help for it now. "They're going to blow the op."

"They're professionals," Robin said. "They'll watch for the hunter and neutralize him if they have to."

"Shouldn't that be your job?"

He swung his golden gaze to the side, eyeing him pointedly. "Someone has to keep eyes on you." Then eyeing his attire, added, "In a suit again, I see."

"In case I have to pretend to be Evan." Daphne would

immediately know it was him, but unless Dyami had paid close attention to his twin's eye color last time or had been in the presence of Evan's magic, he likely wouldn't. No telling if Daphne would tell him; no telling whose side she was on—Chaos or Nature.

Nature, fuck.

"What about—"

"The pack has her covered," Robin said, anticipating his query.

"At my safe house? That everyone knows about now?"

Robin shrugged and shifted his gaze across the street again. "Back to your cousin . . ."

"Maybe she's playing him."

"Or she's playing you. Could she be working with Evan?"

The thought made his stomach churn. "Daphne and Canton were tight." They were the oldest siblings in each family, born only a couple of days apart. They grew up together, worked together, each other's professional partner. "I can't believe she'd betray him or Nature."

Robin was uncharacteristically quiet, as he kept a watchful eye on the café. "How much do you know about Canton's final days?"

Atlas wobbled in his crouch, caught off guard by Robin's question. He braced himself on the parapet wall and let the familiar waves of guilt crash over him. "He went off the grid," Atlas said, recalling those horrible days of nothingness until one night he'd been jarred out of sleep by the sense of imbalance, of falling, like the earth had disappeared out from under his feet. Three blinks to wakefulness later and he'd known his brother was gone. Three weeks later, Daphne had returned with confirmation of his death.

He swallowed hard and shook off the ghosts of that awful time. "But Mary became Nature, and Icarus a vampire, so Canton was successful."

"And then he died."

The simple statement had the definitive tone of consequence, not chronology, and Atlas was knocked off balance once more. "What are you—"

Robin's phone dinged, cutting off Atlas's question. The coyote took one look at the screen and snarled "Fuck."

"What's going on?"

Robin tilted the phone his direction. One look and Atlas's vision went red. In the photo Adam had snapped, Daphne was handing Dyami a sheet of paper with a sketch on it—of Mary. Her hair, her outfit, and her expression were the same as in the vision Daphne had nicked from him.

Was this why Canton had gone dark at the end? Because his best friend, his family, his partner had turned on him? How long had Daphne been working with the enemy? Had some part of Atlas always known and that was why he'd stayed away from home? Why he'd never worked as a team? He knew why when it came to the shifter beside him, why it was easier to hate him than open himself to fate's mercy. But when it came to Daphne, was this what had stopped him from taking Canton's place at her side?

He didn't hesitate, raising his hand to snap, and at the last second, Robin grabbed hold, porting them both through the tear—and into a fight already in progress. Daphne was hurling orbs, keeping Adam and Icarus trapped behind a flipped-over table, while she and Dyami scuttled for the door.

"Can you get her hands?" Atlas whispered low. "Like you did mine at the club?"

"If you can hold those orbs back long enough for me to get behind her."

Atlas couldn't recall the last time he'd seen Daphne's magic, but he was certain it hadn't been swirled green and gray like it was today. There was no yellow in it, not like in Evan's, but there was enough doubt in her mind and magic that Atlas's full-strength conviction easily deflected her orbs. Given the opening, Adam and Icarus chased a fleeing Dyami out the door, while he and Robin advanced on the real traitor in the room. One more blinding blast by Atlas, and an impressive human leap by the shifter—from a bench seat, to a table, to an overhead beam, from which he swung to a landing behind Daphne—and they had her. Robin shoved his fingers through her smaller ones, holding them apart, while Atlas pushed her back against Robin's sturdy frame, a hand circling her throat.

"When did he get to you?" he demanded.

She didn't have to ask who. Yellow flickered in her eyes, streaking through the green, before her once vivid irises faded to dull gray. "When I lost another cousin." She gulped, her words pleading and strained as she forced them out beneath his hand. "We can't keep going like this, Atlas."

His heart ached with sympathy and betrayal. He understood, better than anyone—the exhaustion and loneliness, the ups and too many downs, the never-ending fight. And she'd been fighting it longer than him. Long enough, it seemed, to consider a different path. One that led away from him, from the promises they'd made to their mothers, and from the calling they'd all once served. She'd been a beacon to him, strength and hope in a world that too often seemed hopeless. "I trusted you. I looked up to you."

"Join us." Yellow swirled in the gray. "Let's end this."

End this.

He didn't have a choice. "You know what she looks like."

If Daphne was telling the truth, she'd only just switched sides, but that sense of falling like he'd felt the day Canton had died ripped through Atlas again. Together with another tear in his chest like the day he'd lost his other brother. They'd both known, Canton and Cole. Both going it alone rather than risk the breaking point they knew Daphne had somewhere.

Yet only he was left to find it.

To end this.

"You told me, cuz," she said. "Deep down, you want this to be over too."

A final manipulation, and yet, nothing compared to Atlas's over the past decade, moving pieces around the board to fit his agenda, but today he wasn't the one in the wrong.

"No." Wetness pricked the corners of his eyes, as he pressed more firmly with his hand. "You stole it from me."

"You don't have to keep going like this," she urged him once more.

If only that were true, if only his destiny hadn't been set the day he and Evan were born and cemented for good when the man behind Daphne and his twin sister had come into this world. "I do," Atlas said, voice wavering, his vision wobbly with unshed tears. "It's the name she gave me." He lifted his other hand and cupped her cheek, wiping away the tear that streaked down her own pale cheek, a match to the one racing down his. "I love you," he told her.

"I love you too." She closed her eyes, her final words a whisper. "And I forgive you."

"Thank you," he said, even if he didn't believe there was enough forgiveness in the world to save him. From any of this. He closed his fist around her throat and added another loved one lost to the war.

TEN

Daphne's body had barely dropped between him and Robin when Adam and Icarus came rushing back through the door—sans pretender. "Where's Dyami?" Robin barked.

"Gone," Icarus replied. "Getaway car."

"Fuck!" Atlas cursed, then because he needed to do something with the anger and resentment, the hopelessness, spiraling through him, he shoved Robin in the chest, two-handed. "Why didn't you go after him?"

He gestured at the lifeless witch between them. "Because I was holding her fucking fingers apart. Like you asked me to."

"Dyami knows what she looks like now. I have to—"

"The pack has her." The coyote's calm confidence was the only thing keeping Atlas from flying into a million magical pieces, from giving in to the awful energy raging inside him. Robin glanced past him to the other pair. "Was the hunter ever here?"

Adam flashed a keycard. "Bribed the front desk clerk for it. Let's go find out."

"Did you also tell them to stay out of here?" Atlas asked with a sweep of his hand at the death and destruction surrounding them.

"I have been doing this for a while," the ex-cop deadpanned, before following his partner down the hallway toward the internal staircase leading to the rooms upstairs.

Atlas moved to follow but was stopped by Robin's big hand splayed against his chest. "Channel it."

"I don't know what you're talking about."

"Your magic. It's bordering on chartreuse right now. It's supposed to be moss. Fix it."

"Fix it?" The magic he tried to channel to the hand in the center of his chest hit a brick wall, rebounding on Atlas and causing him to stumble back a step, gasping. "How?"

"You tell me. Later." He moved to block the hallway, arms crossed. "Channel it for now."

It was on the tip of Atlas's tongue to argue, the defensive instinct so ingrained at this point when it came to Robin, but they didn't have time for that today. Not with Dyami and the hunter on the loose, Evan too. He closed his eyes and inhaled deep, smothering the darkness with his mission, his purpose, his vow. When he was steady, his magic no longer pinging around like a reckless pinball, he opened his eyes. Whatever Robin saw there must have been enough, the shifter dropping his arms and turning for the stairs.

Atlas followed him up to the second floor, then to the open door at the end of the hallway. A half step over the threshold and Atlas had to clasp the doorframe to keep the magic he'd just channeled grounded.

"Doesn't look like he was ever here," Icarus said, Atlas hearing him as if in a tunnel.

"But the clerk's description matched," Adam said. "He was here, at least briefly."

"Or someone was magically pretending to be him," Robin said.

Someone like Evan, who'd definitely been here, his magic lingering.

And if Daphne had sent him a quick mental word about Mary's best protectors all being in LP instead of at the safe house, a property Daphne knew about from Cole's final days, then Atlas knew exactly where Evan would be headed.

Fuck. "We need to get out of here."

"We'll search the surrounding area and deal with the body," Adam said, as the ringing in Atlas's ears grew louder.

"The body?" he practically shouted. "She was my cousin." Even if it had been his own hands that had taken her life. Another death in the family he was responsible for. Robin's increasingly, annoyingly familiar hand landed on his shoulder, and Atlas shrugged it off. "Don't touch me," he barked at the dog, before setting his irate sights on the hometown resident in the room. "You don't think anyone will recognize you?" he said to Icarus, same as he had to Mary.

"If they do, they won't understand why I look the same as I did thirty years ago." He flicked a hand at his ginger hair. "And it's the first time I've had my real color since I was ten."

"What about the barber who dyed it the first time?"

Icarus laughed. "The guy at Shorty's in Santa Maria? He was ancient back then. I'm sure he's dead by now."

If he knew Shorty's, then . . . "You remember the cemetery a block over from there?"

He nodded.

"Bury her between her mother and Canton."

Color drained from Icarus's face, and he gulped, his words seemingly caught in his throat. Did the nurse turned vampire turned field medic suddenly have an affliction against dead bodies and graveyards?

Before he could ask, Adam stepped in for his partner. "We'll take care of her and meet you back at the safe house."

"Fuck, Robin," Atlas said, spinning on his heel. "How many people did you tell?"

"The ones who needed to know," he replied. "Who won't try to kill her."

Fair. But dirty. "Fuck you."

Robin brought his hand down on his shoulder once more. "Be mad at me later. Right now, just get us the fuck out of here."

Also fair. And not up for debate. Atlas raised his hand and snapped.

ELEVEN

Atlas ported them to the no-longer-safe house and realized how true his words had become.

A battle was in full swing. Dyami's two casino goons were squared off with Robin's coyote cousin, Jenn, and her mountain lion partner, Abigail. Two other faces Atlas recognized from the casino were trading blows with Brock, one of Vincent's warlocks Adam had turned, and Jason, the hulking smuggler who was Paris's best friend and carried a phoenix with his soul. His skin glowed with the firebird's red and orange heat.

That battle, however, didn't frighten Atlas; he was confident Adam's team could handle Dyami's henchmen. It was the familiar magic that raised his hairs and threatened to unleash his own that caused his pulse to spike.

"Evan's here," he said, and in the space of one breath, in a flash of golden light and cracking bones, Robin shifted, the giant coyote pulling even with Atlas's steps. Together, they slunk from the edge of the vineyard to the shadows of the cottage, approaching the back steps. Then halting when Mary appeared in the loft window above.

Atlas held his breath, certain Evan would appear behind her, would snap her neck as he'd done Daphne's and then Nature would be dead for good. Chaos would reign, with Evan as his vessel, and the world would never be the same, would be over before any of them knew it.

But Evan didn't appear, and the green-haired pixie made a series of hand gestures Atlas vaguely recognized as sign language. Nothing vague about Robin's understanding, though. Golden eyes keen, he nodded his big rusty head, then nudged Atlas's hip with his muzzle, aiming him away from the cottage. "He's not in there with her?"

Robin shook his head, then made a low plaintive whine as he prodded him again, shoving him toward the walkway that led down the hill.

To the main house.

Above which corvids circled, two giant ravens among them, Mac and his younger brother Liam, the current reaper for the Monte Corvo clan.

Atlas's stomach sank.

With no time to waste, he grabbed the dog by the scruff and cut a hole in the plane to the more vulnerable. But they were too late. The green mist had barely faded from around them when Evan appeared in the doorway from the kitchen, an arm curled around the throat of the vineyard manager's preteen son.

"Stay right there, brother," he said, yellow orb hovering at his side.

"Let them go," Atlas said. "They have nothing to do with this."

"On the contrary, I showed up, and they wanted an

update on the battle for Nature. Wanted to know how they could help." He cinched his arm tighter around the trembling boy's neck. "Even this one. Simon, was it?"

The boy's dark, tear-filled gaze strayed toward the kitchen before bouncing back to Atlas and the coyote beside him, Robin's teeth bared.

"Simon," Atlas said, focusing the boy's attention on him. "Are your parents in there?" he asked as gently as the anger gathering in the back of his throat would allow. Twin tears escaped Simon's eyes, streaking down his cheeks, and some of the anger escaped. "They're humans!" Atlas shouted at his brother. "You should've left them out of this."

"They're fodder."

Growling, Robin tensed, every muscle coiled, as if he were about to pounce, but as Evan's orb grew brighter, Atlas put a hand in front of Robin, pausing the impending attack. "Go check the kitchen."

Another low growl but Robin conceded, veering into the adjacent room to confirm the nightmare Simon's tears hinted at.

"Does he know?" Evan asked, and Atlas snapped his gaze back to his suited twin.

"There's been enough death today already." The last thing any of them needed was a fully informed Robin on the rampage.

"I heard you killed our dear cousin."

Simon's eyes grew wide, then wider still at Robin's thunderous howl from the kitchen, loud enough to rattle the windows in the room where they stood. The boy cut his eyes toward the front door, wisely away from the threat supernatural beings posed to humans like him. But every minute Atlas kept his brother talking was another Simon stayed alive. And another for the cavalry swirling above to answer Robin's call.

"Because you preyed on her fears," he said to Evan. "On the losses we've all suffered. Same as Chaos is preying on yours."

"You could join me too. We could share the power, like we were always meant to."

Atlas shook his head, dismissing his brother's corrupted version of fate. "Not like this." From the kitchen, a door slammed and a cacophony of *caws* and *kraas* followed, the cavalry closing in. "You're outnumbered. You can't get to her."

"Maybe I wasn't here for her," he said, then hurled his orb at Atlas.

So much for sharing power.

Atlas blocked the hit with his own orb, diverting Evan's to the cabinet of wine goblets along the wall. Between the shattering glass and the sea of corvids streaming in from the kitchen, Mac's violet-eyed raven at the point, Evan was momentarily distracted, his arm loosening around the boy's neck.

"Simon, get down!" Atlas shouted, before firing an orb of his own at Evan. Then another, buying Robin time to corral Simon. "Get him to the others!"

The coyote didn't argue, sliding across the hardwoods, scooping Simon up with his mass, and carrying him out the door that Atlas blasted open for them. Mac and his flock followed them outside, creating a shield against the enemy, leaving Atlas alone in a face-off with his brother.

"You're their prisoner," Evan said as he spun up another orb. "Nature, fate, our mother and his. You can be free, brother. You don't have to do what they say. You don't have to end up like Canton and Cole."

All the anger that had been gathering in the pit of Atlas's stomach, that had been clawing up his throat and searing through his veins, made the two glowing green orbs above his hands glow brighter, made them powerful enough to end Evan.

But then Robin charged back through the door and drew Evan's attention—and the orbs meant for Atlas.

Atlas had no choice. He didn't want the same fate to befall him that had befallen his twin.

With a final blast of power, he put everything he had into the orbs he hurled at the yellow ones, then hurled himself at Robin, grabbing the dog's tail and snapping them out of there.

TWELVE

They landed back in the crowded safe house to find Nature's army checking each other over for injuries, including Abigail tending to a still trembling Simon. Atlas moved to comfort the boy too but barely made it a step before he was spun back around by the biceps, a post-shift Robin growling in his face. "Why'd you do that?"

"He was going to kill you."

"And now he's going to come up here and kill her and the rest of us."

"He's not," Atlas said, shaking loose of Robin's hold. "Evan would have come after her already if that was his purpose."

"What was it then?" Mary asked from atop the loft stairs. She stood next to Mac, who was cinching the terrycloth robe Atlas had stolen from Icarus around him.

"You need to get somewhere safe," Atlas replied, then said to Mac, "Take her back to Monte Corvo. Non-magically."

"We're not idiots," Jenn grumbled, the bark in her tone

so much like her cousin's that Atlas had to fight a smile. "We took Paris's plane down here."

Atlas's smile fought harder, making his lips twitch. He covered it with a smirk. "Take everyone back with you." When Simon stiffened, Atlas kneeled before him. "Go with them, okay?" The boy hesitated, trembling harder, and Atlas gently clasped his arm, easing some of the anxiety. "They're going to an even bigger vineyard than this one." That notion seemed to comfort him some. "They'll take care of you. And I'll be there before long too. Promise."

The boy gave a small nod and accepted Abigail's offered hand, the shifter leading him toward the front door. Once they were outside, Atlas stood, snatched the framed picture of his brothers off the mantel, then headed the opposite direction, to the back door. "And torch this place on your way out."

It was already burned; might as well make it official. Plus, it was standard operating procedure for erased persons; burn all the evidence. The stone walls would survive, as they had for generations. The rest Atlas couldn't care less about, the only important item in his hand. He let the door slam behind him and set off on the path to the main house, needing to pick up Evan's trail again, hoping there would be enough of his brother's magic left to track.

He made it as far as the corner of the main house when Mister Doesn't Make a Sound caught up with him again. Robin hauled him into the shadows and shoved him back against the stone wall, the picture falling from Atlas's grasp and clattering to the ground. Mister Also Allergic to Clothes paid it no mind, crunching the frame under his bare foot. He pinned Atlas's wrists above his head and loomed over him, invading every inch of his space. Chests pressed together, Robin shoved his thick thigh between his legs and, leaving one rough hand around his pinned wrists, circled his throat with the other.

"What are you doing?" Atlas rasped out against the painful, obnoxiously perfect hold.

"Making sure you're really you."

"What the fuck does that mean?"

"You and Evan were dressed just alike. You *look* just alike. And I left that room."

"For two minutes, at most. And as soon as you were back, you saw my magic."

"How do I know you didn't fake that?" Robin said, voice louder, body pressing impossibly closer. "Didn't make it another color?"

Atlas matched him in resistance and volume, fighting the hold and shouting, "Look at my eyes!"

"Same answer!" the coyote roared back.

With a flick of his fingers, Atlas cast a sparkling green dome around them, from the wall above their hands to the ground beneath their feet, blanketing them in the energy he balanced daily, magic that the man pressed against him could either destroy or fortify, even if he didn't realize it yet. "You know what my magic *feels* like."

Robin's deep-throated growl was a menacing almost-purr that sent goose bumps racing across Atlas's skin. Robin's voice, when he spoke again, sounded as strained as Atlas's cock felt. "What was he talking about fate?"

Atlas tossed another grenade into the conflict; what was one more explosion today? "It's what we do, me and you. We run from fate."

Robin rolled his hips, digging his own stiff cock against Atlas's hip. "Does this feel like running?"

Atlas groaned, his Adam's apple bobbing wildly against the hand still clasped around his throat. This felt like the furthest thing from running, which was what they both should be doing, for their own sakes and humanity's, but fuck if Atlas didn't want to feel more of him.

As if hearing his deepest, darkest desire, Robin released his wrists so he could shove a hand between them, palming Atlas's cock through his pants. "I know what you smell like too." He curled his fingers around his length and stroked, long and slow and hard, eliciting another groan from Atlas. "The real you. Not the decaying stench of dark warlock you put on like you do these fucking suits." He released his cock, and Atlas nearly snapped at him to put his goddamn hand back where it belonged, but caught his words when Robin ripped open his fly instead. That was more like it, and Robin's grin when he found him bare underneath only made Atlas's dick harder. But then the fucking coyote had to go and be a menace, putting impossible conditions on an already agonizing predicament. "Make the stench go away."

"No."

The grip on his throat tightened. "Drop the shield, Atlas."

He shook his head. He'd never admit it to anyone, but he'd wanted Robin's hands on him like this for longer than he could remember. He'd allow himself this much, a quick hate fuck to get their frustrations out, but nothing more. Not the other side of the coin that would destroy them both in the end, the fate he'd spent a lifetime running from. Dropping the scent shield, letting Robin all the way in, was a line Atlas wouldn't—couldn't—cross, for all their sakes.

Robin took him in hand, the rough friction of his

calloused fingers making Atlas's eyes flutter closed. But then Robin shifted the hold around his neck, sliding his hand up to clasp the side of his face, fingers digging painfully against this skin. "If you're not going to drop the smell, then keep these open." He tapped his fingers at the corner of Atlas's eye. "So I know it's you."

Atlas opened his eyes and met the burning gold ones mere inches from his. "You believe me now?"

Robin stroked his length. "You're not faking this."

No, he wasn't. For all the times he had while playing this or that role, he wasn't playing any role today. He was just a needy man being expertly handled by the one person he'd wanted to handle him most. He thrust his hips, shoving his dick into Robin's fist, tunneling through the tight, rough grip.

When Robin took his hand away again, Atlas's anger flared. "Don't you dare leave me hanging again, asshole." The coyote's smirk made his anger flare hotter and the shield around them grow brighter. But then anger ignited into something else searing when Robin clasped his own cock with Atlas's in his fist, the two of them hot and hard together. "Oh, fuck."

"Tell me, Atlas . . ." He added a twist to his stroke, and Atlas thanked all the deities for the thigh holding him up. "Who did this better? Me or that priest in the club the other night?"

Fire tripped through Atlas's veins. "You were watching?"

"Fuck yes," Robin purred, his cock like steel against Atlas's. "And for the record, I like you better in the kilts."

"So do I." Fighting Robin's grip on his face, Atlas

dipped his chin enough to spit on Robin's fist, adding the extra bit of slick and filthy he needed.

"Did you do that the other night?" Robin added his own, the glide of his fist easy now, the only friction each other. "Did you go home, spit in your fist, and fuck it like this?" He thrust hard against him, the stone wall behind Atlas digging against his back. "Were you thinking about me and that bet you've lost?"

Atlas glared at the irresistible menace, and Robin's answering laugh was as sexy as it was irritating. And when he released his face to brace his forearm on the wall behind Atlas, to cushion Atlas's head from the hard stone, Atlas didn't want to think about the pinch in his chest. An obnoxious ache that intensified when Robin pressed their temples together, grunting in Atlas's ear with each stroke toward their climax. That damn near exploded when they spilled together over Robin's fingers, and Robin spilled the sweetest, most terrifying words in his ear. "I'm done letting you hide from me."

Fuck, what would that mean for them, for their allies and enemies, for Nature and Chaos? Robin didn't know the half of it. And he never could. It was easier—and safer—to keep up the not altogether difficult pretense of hate.

To keep running.

Atlas dropped the magic around them and let the cool December air dissipate the heat that had built between them. Let it harden his voice and spine as he rebuilt his walls. "I still hate you."

"I know you do." Robin pushed off the wall, then had the fucking gall to lick his fingers clean. "And you still hate yourself more, same as me."

Thank fuck for the wall holding Atlas up, the sight and

the verbal shot taking his already wobbly knees out completely. And thank fuck Robin had already turned back toward the cottage, tossing a dismissive "Meet us at the mountain" over his shoulder.

Atlas lowered his arms that he'd left above his head against the wall, his fingers free the entire time. Not once during that entire encounter had he ever considered snapping himself out of the coyote's hold.

They were so fucked.

THIRTEEN

Atlas didn't immediately go to Talahalusi like he'd ordered the others.

After catching his breath and cursing himself, he cleaned himself up, then bent to pick up the picture of his brothers.

And the one behind it that had jostled loose when he shook the other free of the broken glass. Two green-eyed women and a third one with golden eyes and honey blond hair, each of their faces split with a smile.

He should burn it, let their secret die here, but that seemed like a push too far, especially on a day when he'd already tempted fate to the max. Folding the photo instead, he hid it inside the other and shoved them both in his wallet, then with a last look at the blazing cottage up the hill, snapped himself to the cemetery where he'd buried another brother eight days ago. He'd been prepared to kneel alone next to the second freshly dug grave but found a familiar form sitting cross-legged between the two, like he was hanging out with friends. Souls the medium could see and hear.

"I know," Paris said with a laugh to one of them. "But I consider him a friend." He twisted half around and threw him a smile. "There you are. Took you long enough."

"Did they take your plane and leave you behind?" Atlas teased as he wove through the Shaw graves to reach his former pupil, as Robin had called him.

"I told them you'd get me home." He looked good, color in his cheeks, brown eyes lively, a wide easy smile. He seemed comfortable in his skin in a way Atlas had never seen the young man. "And I thought you might need a friend."

A knot formed in Atlas's throat, and he swallowed hard to force it down. Paris Cirillo was the one thing he'd done right in this world. Teaching him, sheltering him, believing in him. "You thought wrong."

"Cut the crap, Atlas."

"Oh," Atlas drawled, dramatically rearing back, a hand splayed on his chest. "Growing more of that backbone."

"Thanks to you."

He lowered himself onto the ground beside Paris. "I tried to sacrifice you."

"So did Robin. You both had your reasons."

"That's not—"

Paris bumped a shoulder against his. "I forgive you. Same as I forgave him." Then jutted his chin at the freshly dug grave. "Can you forgive her?"

"Some part of me understands." He propped his elbows on his knees and held his head in his hands, fingers tugging at the roots of his hair. "The things I did at Vincent's side . . ."

"The things my father *made* you do because he had your brother." Atlas whipped his gaze back up. "I saw it," Paris explained.

"I was there voluntarily, at first."

Paris shook his head. "Not voluntarily. You were doing your job. Did you forgive Cole, or Canton, or your mother, for putting all this on you?"

The kid was also growing into that big brain Atlas always knew he had. Wrap all that knowledge and intuition in a blanket of empathy, and it was a powerful combination. He was a perfect medium; Atlas only hated what he'd had to put Paris through to get him there.

He raked a hand through his hair, then let his arms hang over his knees. "I lied before. I am sorry for what I did to you."

"I know you are. I can see it in your aura. I thought Robin won the prize for aura with the most guilt but nope, you're the winner."

Atlas hung his head back and sighed, something else he and the coyote had in common.

"Not gonna tell you what I saw just now."

Atlas chuckled. "Thank you."

Several long moments of comfortable silence passed while Atlas pushed aside the matter of the coyote and searched inside himself for a well of forgiveness that was perilously close to dry. Daphne had forgiven him for what he'd had to do, same as Paris. Could he return the favor? "She could have plunged us into darkness."

"Unless she knew you'd stop that from happening."

"Maybe a part of her thought that, but a bigger part of her wanted out."

"Flip that," Paris said. "Assuming what Liam told me

before he joined the others is true. And I have no reason to doubt him."

Neither did Atlas; the reaper had no reason to lie. And that truth only made Atlas feel worse. He hung his head again and wrapped his hands around his nape, the weight of it all too much to balance.

Paris clasped his shoulder, his touch and words gentle. "Come to the mountain, Atlas. You don't have to keep doing this alone."

Folks kept telling him that, and folks kept dying. For *we*. He couldn't risk the man beside him, the deity they protected, the son of the woman whose picture was in his pocket. "I can't—"

"At least hear us out. At least lay eyes on her there so you know she's safe. Then make your decision. You owe me that much."

Atlas had to laugh at the spunk that had been punched down for so long, that suited Paris so well. "There's that backbone again. No promises."

Paris nodded. "No promises." He stood and brushed off his pants. "I'll give you a minute," he said, then wandered off among the headstones.

Worry instinctively spiked, but then Atlas remembered who the human here was and who the souls in their presence were more likely to protect. With Paris safe, he turned his attention back to the grave in front of him. "I'm sorry," he told her, then tapping that well Paris had somehow filled with just enough of what he needed, added, "I forgive you."

He shifted onto his knees and dug his fingers into the dirt, pouring all his magic into it, all of his real self that only a few people sensed beneath the stench of decay. He propelled blades of grass up through the dirt, growing high and fast enough to match the strips of green on either side of the grave, hiding it within seconds. Her father, their family would simply think Daphne had gone off on another of her "work assignments." Atlas would have Mary forge an email to sell the story. And by the time the truth came out, Atlas would be gone too. "I'll see you soon, cuz."

FOURTEEN

Atlas leaned against the bars of the library cage in the cellar of Mac and Paris's Monte Corvo villa. "I like it better on this side." Two months ago, he'd been on the other side of the bars, pretending to be held captive while trying to convince Mary's forces to stay out of his way. No such luck, seeing as he was right back here. And without a bottle in his hand this time. "Miss the wine, though."

Jenn growled from where she sat at the retired tasting table in the middle of the room.

Robin strolled around the end of the table to the empty chair beside her, resting his forearms on top of it. "He's baiting you."

She twisted in her chair, glaring up at him. "Why aren't you taking it?"

He straightened off the chair back, and for a moment, Atlas thought he was going to claim it, but he just shrugged and continued walking the length of the table, past the end of it, and to a barrel in the far corner. He hitched himself onto it and leaned his torso back against the wall, flannel-clad arms crossed over his chest.

The rest of the team made their way down the stairs and into the room, filling up all the seats except the one beside Jenn, and if Atlas figured right, that last one was for Abigail, not Robin. His friends hadn't fully forgiven him either, especially not Mac, whose wary violet gaze bounced between them.

Abigail was the last person to enter the room.

"How's Simon?" Paris asked from his seat at Mac's side.

"Understandably upset," Abigail said, as she claimed the open chair. "But Pati and Pax are helping."

Atlas swung his gaze to Mary at the head of the table. "You shouldn't all be under one roof."

"We have less than two weeks to Solstice," she answered. "We have no time to waste. Jason and Kai have them. Put up more shields if you think it's necessary."

He pushed off the bars and slowly circled the room, testing the shields that were in place and reinforcing any weak spots, all while listening to the debrief going on at the table, Adam taking lead.

"These are the three main players on the board." He opened a folder and withdrew three photos, spreading them out on the table, one by one. "Evan Shaw, Atlas's twin brother and Chaos's right hand. Dyami, the pretender eagle, Chumash elder for the tribe in Nipomo. And the hunter."

"We know who the first two are," Robin said from his perch. "Who's the hunter?"

"A human," Adam answered.

"Erased," added Icarus, who'd been holed up excavating with his sister all evening.

"He sounds closer to the three of us," Atlas said, gesturing at himself, Mary, and Icarus, indicating the subtle shift in vocal tone that set folks from the South apart from their Northern neighbors. "From what I've gathered, he lost someone about the time of the Rift, maybe multiple someones, and he's been on the warpath ever since, targeting the magical and supernatural."

"So he's a religious zealot?" Icarus said, as he cinched his reclaimed robe around himself.

Atlas shook his head. "He blew up a church harboring paranormals. I barely got everyone out of there. Even my zealot father wouldn't go that far."

"So he wants what?" Mac asked.

"A normal life." Atlas flitted a hand in the air. "Free of all this."

"And he what?" Jenn scoffed. "Thinks if he kills her—"

"And Chaos."

"That magic will disappear, and the world will be one where his loved ones would've lived?"

"They'll still be dead," Abigail said.

"And besides," Mac picked up, "that's not how it works. There are no humans either without Nature."

"And no Nature without Chaos," Atlas finished.

"It's a balancing act," Robin said. He'd been so uncharacteristically quiet that Atlas had almost forgotten he was there, same as everyone else at the table who whipped their gazes his direction. "It always has been."

Paris was the first to twist back around in his chair toward Mary. "But you've been trying to destroy Chaos?"

"Is that what she's been doing?" Atlas challenged, and the pixie tellingly kept her lips sealed.

Everyone around that table thought he was the master

manipulator, and they weren't wrong, but Nature was in a class by herself. She was also right, however; there were too few days until Solstice to get into how inconsequential they all were when the poles of their existence went to war. If he was going to balance their shit so they didn't all die, he needed the table full of people—distractions—occupied and out of his way.

He finished casting his last spell, then slid into the space between Mac and Paris, because yes, he was an asshole. And because Adam, the most strategic of the soldiers around the table, was directly across from them. He pushed the picture of the hunter back toward him. "You take the hunter. He'll be making his way north. I'll give Icarus and Mary everything I know on him. Excavate and track until you find him." He grabbed the picture of Dyami next and pulled it in front of Mac. "You're on Dyami. Use your connections with the tribes and your badge. He's power hungry. He's made other mistakes. I'll turn over what my excavator found. Investigate the licenses at the casinos and bring him down."

Robin hopped off the barrel, his heavy boots *thunk*ing as they hit the floor. "And you'll go after Evan?"

He rotated to face the coyote stalking his direction. "He thinks I'm wavering."

Robin stopped directly in front of him, his golden eyes hard and assessing. "Are you?"

"It's a balancing act," Atlas said. "Every day."

"And if you catch him, will you kill him or use him to bring Chaos through the veil?"

"What if we can do both?" Atlas realized his slip the minute it crossed his lips.

Robin didn't miss the *we* either, his stern face cracking into a victorious smirk. "She promised me revenge."

"You'll get it." Of that, Atlas was certain. Whether any of them survived was a whole other question.

FIFTEEN

Robin did him the courtesy of making noise as he approached for a change, scuffing his booted feet along the sandy path that led from the villa, along the edge of the reflecting pool, to the vista overlook where Atlas stood casting spells to shore up the property's perimeter. "Are the suits gone for good?"

"If I can help it," Atlas replied. On the way to Talahalusi, he and Paris had made a pit stop by the compound of Sunset Hill penthouse condos that now belonged to Paris. Atlas had needed to resupply on essentials, including his kilts. He hadn't brought any suits with him.

"And all is right with the world," Robin lilted, the put-on tone full of sarcasm, as he flopped onto one of the chaises under the overlook's pergola.

All was certainly not right with the world, but Atlas did feel a measure more like himself out of the suits. Reflected in his magic too, the orbs he was lobbing over the vineyards as green as the grape leaves would turn come spring, assuming they won the battle ahead.

Robin stretched his big body out on the chaise, hands pillowed behind his head, eyes closed, leaving Atlas to finish his work, his heartbeat slowing and breaths evening out such that Atlas thought he'd fallen asleep, but as soon as he lowered his arms, the inquisition he'd expected began.

"What does Mary really want?" the coyote asked.

Not the question he expected, but not a surprise either. As far as Robin knew, he was a bystander to this war, a victim who'd lost a loved one, who was trying to save his other friends and family from meeting the same fate. Who was after something far simpler—revenge. Perhaps he was starting to realize his goals and those of the person pulling the strings might not align as he'd understood.

Possibly not as Atlas understood either. "You're the one who's traveled with her the past month."

"You're the one who's been in the shit the past however many years," Robin replied, as Atlas lowered onto the chaise across from him. "How long's it actually been?"

"I can't even remember at this point."

"Were you always on Nature's side?"

He stared up through the pergola's slats at the night sky that was just beginning to lighten, from black to bruised, like he'd been when he'd lost his way. "No."

He expected Robin to want to know all about it, to prove which side he was on now, but the shifter surprised him again, skipping over both those questions to a more painful one. "What brought you back?"

"Who," he corrected, voice a cracked whisper, the truth dismally ironic after the events of yesterday. He rubbed at the center of his chest, trying and failing to make the ache go away. "Daphne."

"I'm sorry you lost her."

The surprising sincerity prompted the same from Atlas. "I'm sorry you lost your sister."

The silence that lingered was a heavy blanket of commiseration, comfortable in its familiarity, awkward to be trapped in it with Robin of all people. While fate had put them on the same side time and again—hell, from the beginning—they'd rarely put themselves there.

"This is weird," Robin said, as if reading his thoughts.

Atlas chuckled. "Don't worry, I still don't like you."

"I don't like you either."

"And no one here likes either of us," Atlas said, recalling the debrief from earlier, Robin relegated to a corner while Atlas tiptoed around folks who wanted to kill him on the regular.

Robin smirked at the sky. "Noticed that, huh?"

"If they're dumb enough to think she didn't decide who went where, then I shouldn't have given them those assignments."

He didn't argue the point. "Mac may never forgive me."

"Even though Paris has?"

"Not good enough. And Adam, well . . ." He raked a hand over his face, but not before Atlas glimpsed the tightening around the corners of his eyes and mouth. "I should have been there that day."

Atlas didn't have to ask what day. He idly wondered what Robin would do if he ever learned the full truth about the day his sister died.

"You didn't answer my question," Robin said, drawing him back to the present. "What's Mary after? What's the endgame this go-round?"

"I don't know," Atlas lied, then told a partial truth. "Pax

is ultimately the answer, but he's too young to do anything about it right now."

Robin wasn't letting him get away with it, shifting on the chaise so he was upright and angled toward him, forearms braced on his knees. "So what do *you* plan to do about it?"

"Make sure Chaos stays trapped on the other side of the veil until Pax is ready." Or trapped somewhere on this side, which was a far more excruciating, far more likely outcome.

"We have to stop Evan."

"One way or another, you'll get your revenge." Either option depended on his last brother being dead by Solstice. What happened after that death, which direction his soul traveled, depended on what side Evan chose when he met his end.

Robin rose from the chaise. "Thank you."

"You're welcome."

"Not for that." He stepped closer, looming over Atlas, stirring memories of what they'd done in the shadows yesterday afternoon. Robin's mind was back then too, only slightly earlier. "For shielding me."

Atlas nodded.

"Why did you?"

The well of things he couldn't name bubbled up again, battling to roll off his tongue. Respect. Commiseration. Desire. Fate. "Because I need a hunter," he said. Also true. "And I hear you're the best."

"At least we can agree on that." He threw a smirk over his shoulder as he turned to leave, and for a brief moment, all did seem right with the world.

SIXTEEN

Three days later, Atlas was ready to murder Robin.

Or fuck him again.

It was a balancing act he was going to lose either way.

And the coyote knew it. What was it he'd said that night at the safe house? He could either drive himself crazy or drive Atlas crazy.

Well, mission fucking accomplished.

Just missing Evan outside of Nipomo, watching him disappear into the crowd at Holy Cross Pier, losing him again after a chase through Portola University, realizing the tip that had led them to Encinal was a wash was all very frustrating.

But not nearly as frustrating as being trapped in motel rooms with a still allergic-to-shirts Robin who regularly walked around with his jeans unbuttoned, no briefs or boxers on underneath. Who prowled around without making a sound, and, like Atlas, somehow disguised his scent. Who showed up the past two mornings with a perfect cup of coffee, like he'd conjured it out of thin air.

He was infuriating, he was maddening, he was everything Atlas wanted and could never fucking keep. And knowing what he sounded like when he came, how rough his voice had been when he'd vowed not to let Atlas hide, what his cock felt like trapped against his, how that big body could cover his made it damn near impossible not to let the madness drive him right back into Robin's arms.

He needed to get out of there before he did something he'd regret, something that would alter the course of the conflict and result in one or both of them dead.

Finishing that morning's perfect cup of joe, he pitched the cup in the tiny trashcan by the scuffed and scratched motel room dresser and headed for the door.

"Where are you going?" Robin asked from his casually lounged position on the bed farthest from the door.

"Out," Atlas said without another tempting look back. "Away from the smell of dog." Robin wasn't reining any of it in today, not his smell, not his heartbeat that too often clocked to his own, and definitely not his throaty chuckle that Atlas slammed the door on.

Outside, he leaned back against the cement wall and inhaled deep, struggling to center himself. *"Whose idea was this?"* he mentally asked his mother. *"Yours or hers?"*

"We decided together."

He rolled his eyes. *"Of course you did."*

"You could let him in."

"I could get him killed. Like his sister."

No reply. She never had an answer for that one.

He inhaled once more, letting the cold air and salty scent of the angry Bay tamp down the boiling frustration. A winter storm had moved through last night, bringing rain, wind, and colder temps, leaving the parking lot full of puddles.

Solstice was growing near; they were running out of time.

Refocused on his mission, he pulled out his phone to start following up with the sources he'd pinged last night after realizing Encinal was a bust. Before he dialed the first source, though, a text appeared onscreen from a North Bay number he didn't recognize. No name, no message, just an address that Atlas mapped to The Corners, a crossroads town further inland, over the ridge and at the foot of Tuysh-tak. Miwok land.

Another text came through. **For Pati. —L.**

Lucy.

How had she gotten his number? What had she over-heard? Questions continued to cascade, his mind racing, and he turned back for the motel room door.

And stopped short.

Did Lucy know who he really was? Or did she think he was someone else? A suited someone else? If he needed to be Evan, he couldn't go in wherever Lucy was sending him with Robin. Or wearing his kilt. They'd lose the advantage of surprise and deception.

But could he afford not to take Robin? Simon would probably be dead if not for Robin; maybe even Atlas. What if Lucy was being held hostage? What if someone had taken her phone and used it to set him up? To send him into a trap?

He needed to thread the needle, to account for both possibilities. Which meant he needed a suit and a head start, and then he'd call in backup.

SEVENTEEN

In the shadow of Tuyshtak, The Corners was a small crossroads village inhabited mostly by the indigenous Miwok. Atlas had rarely strayed this far east. Vincent's criminal doings had been largely confined to YB and Talahalusi. The one time he'd ventured east, to try and steal power from a coven in hiding, it had ultimately led to his death.

Aiming to avoid a similar fate, Atlas withdrew his phone from the pocket of the suit he'd stolen out of another guest's motel room and texted Robin the address of the single-family home he found himself standing in front of. Not the industrial warehouse, saloon, or other commercial building he'd expected. Atlas pushed gently at the aura surrounding the ranch-style home and the generous lot it stood on; no magic that he could detect. He walked up the path to the front door as casually as possible while glancing through the plate glass windows on either side of the front porch. No sign of Lucy, no sign of anyone home, as far as he could tell. No answer to his knock either. Thankful for the cover from the juniper and laurel trees that surrounded the house, he slipped around the side, checking for open doors and windows, peeking through them for any movement or motion detectors in the usual places. Seeing none, he ported himself inside.

And breathed a sigh of relief at not sensing any magic inside either. Ears and eyes open, he slowly worked his way through the home. The house was older but well kept, everything neat, no clutter, no pictures, no personal items whatsoever, the drawers and closets empty. He wouldn't have been surprised to see a For Sale sign in the front yard. It certainly didn't look like Lucy or anyone had been here in some time. Didn't feel or smell like it either, the air stale and cool, no heat on since the temps had begun to drop.

Why had Lucy—or someone—sent him this address? Who did this house belong to? What did it have to do with Pati Miwra? He shot off a text to his excavator as he made his way back to the kitchen, then exited out the back door, only the detached garage left to check.

He approached with caution, the structure behind the house similar in style but not in condition. The windows were papered over, the gutters were full of leaves, and cracks snaked through the structure's exposed foundation. He tried to lift the debris-covered roll-up door. Locked. He circled around to the side and found the single step to the side door broken. The lock on the door, however, was not. Modern and high-tech, its keypad glowed red. He wasn't getting past that in fast fashion, which meant he'd have to port inside blind. Always a risk. He circled the structure, looking and listening for any signs of life. Still nothing, and the state of the place lent itself to the same conclusion. Likely the house was for sale and the owners had shoved all their belongings in the garage, which would be torn down when sold. He contemplated waiting for Robin. The coyote would probably know how to get past the lock, and if there was someone inside, he'd have backup. But it was a small building, one car at most; there couldn't be that many people in there. Atlas could handle them, or at least hold them off long enough for Robin to reach him.

He lifted a hand and snapped.

Into darkness.

Remaining in one place, he extended his senses, listening and smelling, then tentatively poking for any other magic in the space. Finding none, he spun up his own globe as potential defense and to light his surroundings.

The interior of the space was far more akin to the door lock than the structure's exterior. A high-tech monitoring setup like the command room that had been in Vincent's compound lined one wall, a weapons cache the one perpendicular to it, and Atlas assumed the jut out in the far corner was a bathroom given the bed on the other side. The final wall, though, was the one that drew his attention, that called him closer as he tried to make sense of what he was seeing.

An entire wall covered in pictures—of the Shaw family.

Some were the same posed-type shots that Atlas had grown up seeing around the house, including the one of his brothers currently in his pocket. But more were the sort that had been taken at a distance, by someone watching. There were family shots, solo snaps, pictures of each of them at work. Atlas struggled to take it all in, heart pounding, chest tightening, as his gaze bounced from Evan in various states of evil, including standing next to the giant Atlas had killed in LP, to his own arc in photos, from good to evil to seemingly evil, to Cole sneaking into Vincent's compound, what would ultimately prove a life-altering turn of events, to Canton with an arm around a green-haired Mary, the two of them trailing a blue-haired Icarus somewhere, and then a different shot, with Mary standing in between Canton and a snarling Icarus, his fangs extended. Before he could wonder long on when exactly that photo was taken, what exactly had transpired before and after that snapshot in time, his gaze strayed to the last collection of photos, the biggest.

Of his father.

At home, in town, at church, at Cole's funeral two weeks ago.

What the fuck was this? Whose was this? Holding his globe aloft, he made another slow sweep of the space, his gaze passing then speeding back to a familiar sight on the weapons wall.

A crossbow he'd seen a week ago in La Purisima—on the hunter's shoulder.

Was that who this place belonged to? Was the hunter not after magical beings in general, but the Shaws in particular? Was his father the ultimate target?

He needed to have a much longer conversation with his excavator, and he needed another set of eyes on this. With Nature and Chaos on the brink of full-out war, a third-party variable like this was the last thing Atlas needed.

Lifting his phone, he switched the camera to video, held his globe close to the wall, and made a slow survey of the photo collage first, then standing back in the center of the room, made a slow circle to capture it all.

Finished, he clicked back to the text he'd sent Robin earlier and sent another: **ETA?** When it remained on Delivered, not switching to Read, he figured Robin was on paw.

He moved to extinguish his globe and snap back outside, but stopped himself short, one photo in particular calling him back. He snatched it off the wall, pocketed it with the others, then, putting out his globe, ported himself back onto the lawn.

And into the enemy's hands.

EIGHTEEN

They were waiting for him on the lawn. Three henchmen this time, a bobcat shifter who was new to Atlas and two humans he recognized from Dyami's casino. They'd been dressed as dealers that day, but their bulging biceps and thighs had given them away as more than croupiers.

The bobcat sprang first, slamming into Atlas and taking him down face-first, his chest to the ground, the cat on his back. The relatively smaller of the other two men bagged his head and the big one tied his hands. They didn't, however, separate his fingers, and as the trio marched him around the garage toward the driveway, Atlas contemplated snapping himself free.

He stopped himself short again. This was an opportunity to learn more about Dyami's role in all this. Were they taking him to the pretender? Would he finally get a meet? Could he convince Dyami that he wanted to take Daphne's place? Were they holding Lucy hostage? Was Dyami working with the hunter?

His mind was swimming with questions, with possibilities and tactics, while the rest of him was drowning with fear. If he ported himself away, only for Robin to show up moments later, how would the coyote fare in a three-on-one battle? Atlas had no reason to think Robin couldn't hold his own, but could Atlas take that risk? He didn't have to think twice about that answer. Yet even as he committed to the action, allowing Dyami's goons to shove him into the back of what felt and sounded like a utility van, he worried about the fallout. What would Robin think when he found him gone? What the fuck would he do?

"Get in there," one of the humans said, shoving him to the van floor and using his foot to kick him to one side. Atlas shimmied away from the boot, across the grooved metal floor until his back hit shelving, the smell of paint and chemicals stinging his nose.

His nose.

Scent.

Fuck.

He'd spent a lifetime avoiding this, running from it, but what choice did he have in the current situation? Absolutely none. His best hope was that a little would be enough for Robin to lock onto but not enough to give fate the win. Not yet.

He flicked his fingers, casting a tendril of his scent, the real one, along the metal floor and out the drainage grooves beneath the van's back doors.

"This is the guy, right?" said the human who'd shoved him earlier. To make room on a bench seat by the sound of it. "The one Dyami put a bounty out on?"

"Yeah," said the other human from farther away, near where the driver should be. "That's him. Call the eagle and let him know."

A stretch of silence followed during which Atlas idly wondered how much the price on his head was up to—and did Robin know?—before the goon closest to him spoke again. "We got him," he said to Dyami, Atlas assumed. "He was at Cyrus's place. Right where Lucy sent him."

Cyrus. A name to go with the nightmare.

"You're going to let her go, right?" said a new voice from beside the first one. "She did what you asked. I'll keep her in line now, I swear."

The new husband, then—and the shifter, back in human form. He sounded distressed, the promise one of appeasement, but Atlas would have to be convinced that—

A loud crash sounded against the van roof, and the vehicle teetered onto two wheels, sending paint cans flying off the racks and Atlas sliding into a pair of shins. He tucked his head, protecting himself from kicks or cans, just in time as the driver overcorrected, the van teetering the opposite direction, jostling the other two men in the back.

A knee landed in his back, another in his shoulder, and then fuck if one of the assholes didn't use his calf to leverage himself up.

"What the hell, Duncan?" shouted the human. "Sit this van down!"

"What's going on?" echoed the husband.

Duncan, the driver apparently, got the van back on four wheels, skidding to a stop, but before he could answer either question, a familiar roar Atlas shook the van's walls.

"It's that fucking coyote," Duncan hollered. "The bounty hunter one."

"You need to shift again," said the other human to Lucy's husband. "We need this money."

"Not unless you guarantee Lucy's safety," he bargained.

"And I get half the payout." Shrewd, Atlas conceded, but maybe not the time to push his luck.

"Yes, fuck, fine!" Duncan agreed. "Just shift and get rid of the fucking dog."

Magic sizzled inside the van, bones cracked, and a moment later, the bobcat growled. The back doors flew open, claws scraped across metal, and the cat barely got out a fighting hiss before it howled in unmistakable pain.

"Fuck, Duncan!" the other human yelled. "Just leave him!"

Atlas flicked his fingers, the hood and bindings disappearing, and he hurled an orb forward, jamming the gear shift back into park before it broke out the front windshield. Robin leapt through the opening the next instant, jaws open wide for Duncan's neck. Blood splattered across the front seats, and the other man standing astride Atlas tripped over himself and Atlas in his haste to flee the opposite direction, practically falling out the van's back door.

Atlas sent an orb slamming into his back, making sure he'd never get up again.

A bark behind him was all the warning Atlas got before Robin went rushing past him, hurtling out the open doors toward the bobcat who was trying to stagger up. Robin landed on all fours above him, batting him back down and letting out another thunderous roar, his intention clear.

"Robin, wait!" Atlas shouted, as he jumped down from the van and sprinted after him. "They're holding his wife hostage."

Under Robin, the bobcat rolled onto his back and presented his belly, and in the space of a breath, Robin shifted back into human form. He didn't release the cat, though, continuing to hold him down by the neck. Atlas had never heard his voice so menacing as when he leaned down and whispered in Lucy's husband's ear, "Tell whomever you're working for, whomever needs to hear it, that he's mine."

Heat raced down Atlas's spine and fast on its heels was dread, chilling him to his core. So much for only a little.

Robin stalked past him without so much as a look or a word, and Atlas, figuring he needed a minute to cool off, kneeled beside Lucy's husband instead. He spoke as gently as the war of emotions climbing up his throat would allow. "Get Lucy and take her back to her people. Stay there. Do you understand?"

The cat nodded with a whimper.

Straightening, Atlas followed Robin's scent around to the front of the van.

Naked in the midday sun was not a bad look on him. Atlas opened his mouth to make a snide comment to the contrary, or snipe about Robin being late, anything to build up the wall of hate he was desperately clinging to, but Robin beat him to it, hand raised and eyes burning gold. "Not a fucking word." He grabbed hold of Atlas's arm. "You know the distillery tasting room in YB we use as a base?"

Of course he did. He nodded, not saying a word, keeping to the volatile shifter's directive.

Robin tightened his grip, hard enough to bruise. "Take us there. Now."

NINETEEN

Atlas stood in the alley behind the seemingly shuttered tasting room, admiring Robin's bare ass, his firm round cheeks dusted with fine blond hairs that were afire with the midday sun. Atlas looked his fill while Robin unlocked the door, gawking far easier than dealing with what had just happened, what Robin had just said to Lucy's husband.

Mine.

Robin's muscles bunched as he pushed open the metal door and stepped inside. Then let the heavy thing swing right back in Atlas's face. "Hey!" Atlas protested, using both hands to stop the steel weight. Barely.

"Watch the door," Robin called back. "It's heavy."

"No fucking shit." Heaving the door open enough to slip inside, he cringed as the metal scraped across the floor again on its way to closed. Keeping their presence quiet from anyone in the building's other units would be impossible, though from the outside, those other units had looked as deserted as this one. When he turned around, Robin was gone, but his steps and heartbeats echoed from the front of the boarded-up shop. Orb lighting his way, Atlas followed the sounds, distracting himself by peeking into rooms—an office, a bathroom—and taking stock of the crates—weapons, first aid supplies, electronics—and barrels—whiskey, as far as he could smell—that crowded the narrow hall. Before he reached the end, he nearly collided with Robin who, with jeans and a flannel in hand, careened around the corner without so much as an *excuse me.*

"Since when are you not just gonna prance around naked?" Atlas called after his fleeing backside.

And got no reply, Robin ducking into the bathroom and slamming the door shut behind him. When running water started a moment later, Atlas let the angry coyote be and ambled into the main tasting room instead. There was enough light sneaking in around the edges of the boarded-up windows that he didn't need his magic to get a good look at the place. There was a bar off to the right, nothing on the backbar shelves, only a smattering of bottles and glasses on the bar itself. Several square tables were pushed together along another wall, a tangle of cords beneath them, a tech setup for whomever needed it. There were several other chairs around the room, another table he tossed his suit jacket onto, and on the far wall, in the shadows, a chaise. On the floor beside it, denim and flannel spilled out of an open duffel.

Had Robin been staying here at some point? Was this a pit stop on the way to Monte Corvo so he could pick up his things?

Atlas was tempted to go poking through the bag, but as the bathroom toilet flushed, he abandoned that one-way ticket to an even angrier coyote and diverted to the bar instead. Turning over two clean glasses, he filled them with the vodka he found in the underbar fridge and held out a glass to Robin when he returned.

"Why didn't we just go to Monte Corvo?" he asked. A direct question he wanted the answer to and an indirect one to extract a possible explanation for his other observations.

Robin threw back the shot, slammed the glass on the bar, then stepped closer, trapping Atlas between the bar and the barstool behind him. "We didn't go to the mountain yet because I haven't decided whether I need to kill you and dump your body in the Canyon Lands."

Atlas raised a hand, but Robin beat him to the snap, threading his thick fingers between his and pining his hand to the bar. Atlas dropped the glass in his other one, but Robin didn't take the shattering bait. Grabbing that hand too, he twisted it up between them, fingers shoved between his, and splaying their joined hands over his chest. "Eh, eh, eh," Robin chided. "See, I can't decide if you're more dangerous to the cause or the whole fucking key to it, and that's the fucking rub."

He'd known Robin was pissed after The Corners. He'd torn that van apart, torn Duncan apart, and would have done the same to Lucy's husband if Atlas hadn't stopped him. Maybe he shouldn't have, given where the convo had gone.

Mine.

Atlas had one distraction left. He rolled his hips, his own cock half hard from the proximity, Robin's semi likewise poking Atlas's hip. "Is that the only rub?"

"We're not doing that right now," Robin gritted out.

"Oh, so now this is only on your terms?"

"Be fucking serious." Robin squeezed his fingers. "Why

did you leave?" The danger and desperation in his tone warranted an answer.

Atlas gave him the bare minimum. "I got a tip."

"But you didn't tell me?"

"I sent you a text!"

"After you left! We"—he moved their clasped hands between them, Atlas's knuckles first tapping his chest, then Robin's tapping Atlas's—"are a team."

Atlas straightened his back and lifted his chin, pushing back at the glaring coyote. "I already told you, I don't do *we*."

"Then why'd you text at all?"

"In case they were holding Lucy hostage, like they did Simon, and I needed backup."

Robin erased the last inch of space between them. "Is that the only reason?"

The answer to that question was too complicated and too simple all at once . . . *Mine*. Atlas pressed his lips together to keep the truth from spilling out.

Robin growled. "You need to fucking convince me not to kill you right now."

Again, the bare minimum. "I know Evan better than any of you."

"And yet you haven't stopped him in how many years?"

"He knows me better than anyone too."

It didn't have to be that way; the man holding him pinned could change that, if Atlas let him.

If Robin even wanted that, and at the present juncture, he seemed far keener on violence, on the revenge he'd been seeking all these years. "You and your brothers are playing a game, using my friends and family—*innocents*—as pieces, and we keep getting killed."

"And *she* doesn't do the same thing?"

"*She* isn't my concern right now. You are the one who went off alone. To the meet in LP and to the one this morning." He clenched his fingers around his. "And fucking hell, Atlas, I think you get it." Desperation overtook the danger in his tone and words. "You understand that neither of them, Nature or Chaos, are the endgame, that it's a balancing act, and if you fucking die, this whole thing falls apart."

The same was true for him, whether he realized it yet or not.

Mine.

Robin dipped his chin and nuzzled behind Atlas's ear. "You let me smell you." A growled purr laced with agony sent a full body shiver rippling through Atlas. "You cannot risk yourself anymore."

"Why?" he asked on a stuttered breath, wanting to hear that word again in Robin's broken timbre, wanting it to drown out the cackle of fate in his head.

Releasing the hand pinning his to the bar, Robin grasped his face and held them nose to nose, his golden gaze boring into Atlas's. "Because you're mine."

He may have been angry, but Robin still wanted, as much as Atlas. Maybe more. Heat raced down Atlas's spine, from the tips of Robin's fingers digging into his cheek to his stiff cock wedged between them.

Fuck it.

Atlas had sealed their fate the second he'd cast his scent into the wind for Robin to track. To lock onto. He could keep fighting this, keep trying to balance it all himself, keep putting them both in jeopardy by keeping Robin on the outside. Or he could let Robin in and protect him from the inside.

They could both get what they wanted, fools diving headfirst into foolishness.

With his free hand, he covered Robin's on his face and increased the pressure of his hold, just on the edge of painful, just the way Atlas liked it. "Are you going to keep barking at me, or are you going to fucking kiss me like you've always wanted? Like we were always meant to."

Robin's answering growl shook the walls.

His kiss shook Atlas to his core.

TWENTY

Chapped lips, rough stubble, a demanding tongue that forced open Atlas's mouth.

Taking, claiming, devouring.

Using the grip on his face to adjust the angle then diving in for more.

Atlas groaned, caught between turned on and frustrated, melting and fighting. As was usually the case with Robin, the latter won, Atlas taking over the kiss by sucking Robin's tongue deeper into his mouth and pulling him impossibly closer, forcing that big body to stretch the length of his as he leaned back over the arm of the barstool.

They slid together—tongues, bodies, desire.

Short-circuiting reason and filling empty caverns Atlas hadn't realized existed.

When Robin withdrew his tongue for a gulp of air, Atlas let him have two before grabbing the front of his shirt and exerting more control, yanking him back close and taking his turn in Robin's mouth, tongue sweeping through. He tasted wild and hungry, as irresistible as Atlas had always feared. The sadness—the guilt—underpinning it all dreadfully familiar. Atlas wanted to erase it as much for Robin as for himself.

Fuck, this was a terrible idea, and yet Atlas had zero will to stop it, no idea how to even do that. He went back for more, over and over; the first real kiss he'd had in ages—not a show, not an act, not a hold your nose until it's over farce—was making his head spin, his insides tangle, and his cock ache.

He rolled his hips, chasing friction, and when Robin rolled his back, cocks rutting together, Atlas tore his mouth away and panted, just shy of a whine. "Robin, I need . . ." The rest of his words died on a groan, Robin clasping one of his ass cheeks and jerking him higher, a thigh between his legs for Atlas to grind down on, giving him what he needed. He let his head fall back, eyes slipping closed as he rutted. Harder as Robin licked a stripe up his throat. "Fuck yes."

Atlas threaded his fingers through Robin's rusty blond locks, and damn if they weren't softer than they looked. He palmed Robin's scalp, holding his face against his neck as he rode his leg, regretting his pants more with each thrust.

"Last time I'm going to say this," Robin rumbled against his neck, the movement of his rough lips on skin giving Atlas goose bumps and all sorts of mental images. "No more suits."

"But what if I need—"

He shoved back against Atlas's hand, righting his head and looking him dead in the eye. "Wouldn't you rather be humping my leg bare right now?"

Atlas pressed his lips together rather than tell the asshole he'd read his mind.

Robin smirked. "You can't give me anything, can you?"

"I'm about to give you my hole."

And smirk gone, replaced by pure fire in his golden eyes. The suit was practically gone a second later, Robin ripping the shirt down the middle, sending buttons flying, before he likewise ripped the pants from the waist to the middle of one leg. "This isn't even a good one," he snarled.

"I stole it from the motel room two over," Atlas said, as he ditched the remains of the shirt. "I had to make do."

Robin splayed a hand on his chest, fingers drifting across his pecs, from one nipple to the other, making Atlas quake in his arms. "The next time I fuck you—"

"Getting ahead of yourself—"

Robin's leg disappeared, Atlas lost his words in the drop back to his heels, then lost his breath when Robin spun him toward the barstool and, hand in the middle of the back, forced him to bend over the seat. "The next time I fuck you," he repeated, "I want to flip up your kilt"—he ripped the pants the rest of the way off—"suck your cock"—the sucking sound he made around what Atlas glanced over his shoulder to see were two fingers shoved in his sinful mouth —"then fill this hole"—which he then shoved into his hole, Atlas gasping with pleasure and pain—"with your own come before I fill it with mine." Atlas melted over the barstool. "And when I'm done, I'm going to tongue fuck you until you come again."

And melted some more, his mind supplying the pictures to go with Robin's words, his knees weak at the thought alone, his rock-hard cock leaking precome down the inside of his leg.

"Now, are you gonna wear a suit again?"

Atlas shook his head, words too hard to come by.

"And you better be bare under that kilt for me."

"If I mean to have sex." The reply came reflexively, as did the gasp when Robin added another finger, stuffing him full.

"You gonna turn this down?" He pumped inside him, and Atlas keened, so close to the edge, pushing back on Robin's fingers for more. But it wasn't enough, wasn't what he needed to fill all the empty caverns.

"Robin, I need . . ."

As if reading his thoughts again, Robin hauled him off the barstool and spun him around, holding him by the throat until he was steady on his feet. Only to coast his hand down, along the center line of his chest, over his abs, and along the trail of coarse hair that led to the thatch of dark blond curls around his cock. He curled his fingers around the base of Atlas's cock, then made a long, agonizing stroke down the length of him, fingers trailing off at the end, precome dripping from his fingertips. "Not helping," Atlas grumbled, knees weak again.

Robin chuckled. "Not much longer, I promise." He turned on his heel, shedding clothes as he made his way across the room. He was naked when he lowered himself onto the chaise, in that same fucking relaxed posture that had driven Atlas mad all week. Arm stretched across the chaise back, legs spread, his fat cock ready and waiting. "Come here," he rumbled, and not even fate's *I told you so* could have stopped Atlas from crossing that room, especially not when Robin spit in his hand and stroked himself, spreading moisture down his length, getting himself ready.

Atlas didn't hesitate to crawl onto his lap, knees on either side of his hips, fingers coasting through the dusting of red-gold hairs on his broad chest. He leaned forward to nip at the freckled skin that had so tempted and teased him, that was even warmer than he'd imagined. "That was mean."

Robin stopped him short, hand holding him by the face again, the pressure exactly right this time. "I'm not a nice person," he said. "Neither are you. We accept that about each other."

"So how mean are you going to be?"

"I'm not going to touch your pretty cock. You're going to sit on my dick and make yourself come." He tilted Atlas's face down, their lips brushing. "Use me."

Atlas grinned against his lips. "We may have to work on your definition of *mean*."

Robin's palm came down hard against his ass cheek. "Less talking, more riding."

His lips wanted to curl into a wider smile, but he busied his mouth with Robin's for another deep, sweeping taste before he reared back and rose on his knees. Hand around Robin's cock for position, he slowly slid down the length of him, inch by torturous inch, until he was fully seated, stuffed full of Robin.

The shifter leaned back his head, and his thunderous moan nearly made Atlas come on the spot. When he was sure the brush of the coarse hairs that bisected Robin's pelvis wouldn't make him explode, he tipped forward, arms outstretched, hands on either side of Robin's head and nibbled a path up his neck to his ear. "You ready?"

"Now, who's being mean?"

"I'll show you fucking mean." Curling his fingers around the top of the chaise for leverage, he rose to the tip end of Robin's cock, then rammed himself back onto it. Over and over, building them up, Robin's rough grunts in his ear as good as any sweet words, his fingers leaving bruises on his hip and shoulder as he slammed him down harder better than any soft touches, his growled "Mine" as they raced toward their climax almost enough to throw Atlas over the edge.

He reared up one last time and clasped Robin's face, forcing his golden gaze back to his. "It cuts both ways. You get that, right?"

Robin covered his hand, digging his fingers in harder, same as Atlas had done his earlier. "Yours."

Heat and something else exploded inside Atlas, and as he shoved back a final time, his orgasm erupting, Robin's doing the same inside him, he tipped back his head, let his eyes slip closed, and told a cackling fate to fuck right off.

TWENTY-ONE

Atlas kicked the shredded stolen suit aside as he returned from the bathroom. "You know, I have nothing to wear out of here now."

"You can borrow some jeans and a flannel," Robin said from where he stood by the bar.

Atlas made a retching sound, then promptly erased the horrific thought with the shot of vodka Robin offered him.

The coyote eyed him over the rim of his own glass, gaze heated even after round-Atlas-had-lost count. "Tie the flannel around your waist, like a kilt."

An admittedly less horrific idea, but the implications . . . "If I walk into Monte Corvo with your flannel around my hips, they'll know we fucked."

Robin shrugged, tossed back the rest of his vodka, then wound an arm around his middle. He pulled him closer, nose nuzzling behind his ear, semi nudging his hip, ramping up to go again. "Speaking of fucking . . ."

They'd get there—impossible not to with the both of

them still naked—but Robin's comment had piqued Atlas's earlier curiosity again. "Have you been staying here?"

He promptly unplastered himself from Atlas's side and poured another shot. "Between Icarus's shit and Paris's." He rotated to rest back against the bar, gaze toward the boarded-up windows as if he could somehow see outside. "We needed eyes on the city." Atlas didn't think that was all there was to it, given the tightness of his shoulders and the lines that deepened around the corners of his eyes. "And I like it better here."

"Aren't you supposed to love the wide-open range? Roaming the hills and valleys and shit?"

Robin chuckled, his shoulders loosening, and Atlas was glad for it. "It makes me antsy."

"Same," Atlas said, hiding his smile in his glass. "I loathed working for Vincent, but I enjoyed living in YB."

Robin cut him a side-eye and returned a version of his earlier question. "Aren't *you* supposed to love nature? You bought a vineyard, for fuck's sake."

His turn to laugh. "I do, when I just want to be. No mission, no to-do list, no crisis to avert. But when I need to work, I like the challenge of the city. What's more impressive than a weed fighting to grow through a crack in the concrete?"

"You mean Paris," the shifter astutely surmised. Atlas shrugged and finished his shot. "I feel the same," Robin continued. "Running comes naturally, but hunting here in the city, any city for that matter, takes more than speed and strength."

"Strategy."

"Exactly." Robin finished his drink, then angled again

toward Atlas. "It's what we need to do if we're going to survive the next nine days."

He'd walked right into that one, tricky bastard. "I don't do—"

Robin's mouth stole the rest of his protest, drowned it with another of those toe-curling kisses that tangled his insides. "You lost the right to that excuse five fucks ago." Arm around his shoulders, Robin brought them front to front again and buried his nose in the divot behind his ear. "And when you let me smell the real you. Fuck, it's addictive."

He arched his neck, wanting more, Robin's rough lips and teasing touch ramping him up again too. "What do you smell?"

"Spring, in the dead of winter."

Atlas shivered for a different reason; Robin had him dead to rights.

"We have to stop running," Robin said as he withdrew his face from the crook of his neck. "We stop chasing you, you stop chasing Evan, and we work together to catch him and stop Chaos."

"Robin—"

The coyote lifted a hand to his face, palm cupping his cheek, the touch so gentle, so earnest, so unlike the rough touches of earlier, that Atlas nearly whimpered. He didn't know what to do with this Robin nor what to do with his own twisted insides. "Stop fucking running, Atlas. For the sake of all of us and for the sake of your soul."

"You can't run from yours either."

Robin shifted them so Atlas's back was against the bar, to argue more or bend him backward over it, Atlas guessed, but the shifter surprised him, making him gasp when he hoisted him onto the bar top and stood between his spread legs, hands splayed on his inner thighs. "What do you think I'm doing here?" he said, golden eyes smirking up at him. "Now, about that bet you've lost six times over. Make it seven." He didn't wait for a reply before he lowered his head and took Atlas's cock to the back of his throat, stealing Atlas's next breath and silencing any further arguments over *we*.

PART TWO

ROBIN

TWENTY-TWO

Mate was Robin's first thought when he woke.

Gone followed fast on its heels, Atlas absent from the bed they'd made on the tasting room floor.

Robin shot to his feet, pulse racing, senses on high alert. The early morning light was weak around the boarded windows, but he didn't need it, his eyesight more than capable in the dark. His sense of smell too, only a faint trace of Atlas on the air.

He grabbed his phone off the chaise, checking for texts. Nothing.

He nearly hurled it across the room. That fucker had left.

Again.

After everything they'd said last night. After everything they'd done.

Robin wasn't one for sentiment, but he'd thought they'd reached an agreement—a truce, at the very least—where their common purpose was concerned. And an acknowledgment, acted on if not plainly spoken, as to what magic had made them to each other. What the two of them had finally given in to after months—years—of fighting it.

He sank onto the chaise, elbows propped on his knees and head held in his hands. Atlas Fucking Shaw, of all people. He'd sensed a connection the first time he'd been in the supposedly evil warlock's presence. Had written it off as instinct, his coyote recognizing a threat. And Atlas was. Just not in the way Robin had initially thought.

He'd never even considered that Atlas could be the mate his mother had told him about in her letters, the match he'd spent a lifetime running from, being tied to one person as antsy making as the hills and valleys where he'd grown up.

Hell, after Deb's death, he'd used Atlas as the boogeyman, the excuse for his long absences, his erratic behavior, his swings from angry to angrier. But pieces of the puzzle had shifted over the past two months, painting a different picture.

Atlas helping to save Adam and Icarus.

Atlas protecting Mary from Vincent.

Atlas slaying giants allied with Chaos.

Atlas practically raising Paris.

Evan—not Atlas—killing Deborah.

And when Robin had gotten a whiff of the real Atlas beneath the stench he wore like a mask, same as those fucking suits, the connection he'd always sensed, the instinct his coyote had misunderstood, came into focus. Sharpened to a vicious point yesterday when Atlas had cast a tendril of his scent into the wind for him to track.

Mate.

Gone.

Fuck.

He shot out a hand for his phone again, but before he fired off the *Where the fuck are you?* text, the lock on the back door disengaged.

He told the magic inside him to quiet, to disguise his presence from any foe who might enter. Only friendlies should know the code, but he knew enough hackers to accept that an electronic lock wasn't one hundred percent secure. He slid off the chaise into a crouch, prepared to shift if a foe walked through the door, but then coffee and spring tickled his nose and the *who* was no longer a question.

Whether to shift, however . . . Robin was tempted to let the coyote out just so he could roar in Atlas's face for fucking leaving. He was tempted to do something else entirely, though, when the infuriating fucker appeared at the opening to the tasting room, two coffees in hand, with Robin's favorite flannel tied around his waist.

Robin growled as he straightened, no part of it anger, all of it hunger for the sexy blond—his mate—wearing his clothes.

Atlas strolled casually across the room, seemingly oblivious to the fact he'd caused Robin a coronary one second and a boner the next, to the fact his high and tight ass wrapped in plaid was Robin's new favorite target. He set one cup down on the table and sipped from the other, the heat from the drink giving his pale cheeks a lovely blush. "Did you run back here the past two mornings to get us coffee?"

Busted. "How'd you find the place?"

"Followed my nose."

Robin's nose was leading him straight to Atlas's side. He tugged at the knotted sleeves holding the flannel around Atlas's hips. "This works. I like my idea."

"I can tell," Atlas said with a flick of his gaze to where Robin's erection was poking his hip. "But we don't have time for that."

Robin begged to differ. He slipped a hand beneath the flannel to fondle Atlas's gloriously bare balls. Turned out the warlock obeyed some orders. "Do you remember—"

"Yes, I fucking remember," he snapped in that haughty tone that pissed Robin the hell off ninety-nine percent of the time. But that other one percent, when Robin had his hands on him, it turned him the fuck on. "I would love nothing more than to bend over this table and let you shove that fat cock inside me again, but we have to go."

Robin huffed and withdrew his hand.

"Don't pout," Atlas said. "It's unattractive." The smile turning up the corners of his lips said otherwise.

"Liar."

Atlas didn't argue, dodging instead as he strolled with his cup to the chaise and toed the duffel on the floor there. "Get dressed."

He'd rather drink is coffee first. "Where are we going?" he asked between sips of his favorite brew from the only shop left in the Lost Valley.

"Talahalusi. I already called her. She's bringing everyone in."

Whatever Atlas wanted to discuss with the team had to be serious, if he was the one who'd reached out. Maybe what had happened between them last night, what Robin had said about running, had sunk in—for both of them. Robin drained his coffee and tossed the empty cup behind the bar. "What's going on?"

"I know how to find my brother."

"How's that?"

"After that stunt of yours at The Corners yesterday, he knows I'm yours." Tossing his own empty the same direction as Robin's, Atlas closed the distance between them, their breaths mingling as they stood chest to chest, nose to nose. "Now we have to remind him you're also a traitor."

TWENTY-THREE

Jenn propped herself against the cellar wall beside him. "He's wearing your shirt as a kilt."

And Atlas looked damn good doing so. Robin had offered to stop by his condo or to ride along on a snap to wherever else he kept a stockpile of tartans, but the warlock had refused. Robin wasn't mad about it. "I know."

His cousin lowered her voice. "You fucked him."

One corner of his mouth crept up. "I know."

Lower still. "He's the fucking enemy."

The other corner of his lips tried to tip up, but he bit the inside of his cheek to stop it. "I know."

She whipped her gaze to him, strands of honey blond hair escaping her ponytail. "Would you stop—"

"I know it's driving you nuts." His cousin was, second only to Atlas, the easiest of targets to rile up.

Her growl faltered when he let loose his smile, her own resigned chuckle following. "The way you two fight, I guess part of me always knew it was coming."

He waggled his brows. "You know who else was coming last night . . ."

She rolled her golden eyes and backhanded his gut. "Did you get it out of your system?" she asked, as the rest of the team filled the room and claimed their seats at the tasting table.

Robin's smile faded as his gaze sought his mate across the room, the last person he ever thought he'd be tied to, the person he wanted to fuck and strangle in equal measure. "I don't think I'm ever getting him out of my system," he replied, and Jenn gasped, correctly interpreting his meaning. "Trust me," he added, "no one hates that more than me."

Not the sex he'd spent all night having. Not even the fact that he and Atlas seemed to be on the same page for a change, working together to catch Evan and defeat Chaos. But after that mission was done, was Robin ready to have a mate? He'd been a lone wolf the past thirty years. Yes, he had the team here, friends and at least one family member who hadn't shunned him completely, but he was on the outside looking in. Always had been, even before Deborah had died. She'd been his connection to the people around the table; without her, the threads still tying them together were no less heartfelt but all the more tenuous. He'd put his life on the line for any of them, he'd made Deborah that promise, and he acknowledged the world was a better place with all of them in it, even Icarus despite how much the mouthy courtesan exasperated him, but he'd rather hide out in the distillery alone than stay here and sing kumbaya. And he sensed every friend around the table and even the cousin beside him would rather he stay there too.

He deserved that for what he'd done—or rather hadn't.

And it was easier to not disappoint anyone if he kept everyone out.

But he couldn't keep his mate out. While he missed having someone in his life like Deborah, someone who had known him inside and out, he valued his independence more. Valued his free will the most. Was this magic that had tied him and Atlas together, that his mother had told him in her letters would find him when Nature needed him most, overriding that will? He meant what he'd told Atlas last night; he was tired of being a pawn in other people's games —the warlock's, Nature's, magic's. But was the draw he felt toward Atlas, even when he'd hated him most—the blood rushing in his veins, the tightening of his gut, the warmth in his chest, the stiffness of his cock—magic or something else entirely?

Robin didn't like either answer. Hated that it didn't matter even more.

He'd told Atlas to stop running. Could he ignore his own instinct to do the same?

Mac, dressed for a day at the office no matter the location, was the last team member to join them, the scrape of his chair across the floor drawing Robin out of his head and back into the room. "All right, we're all here, again," the raven said, droll as always.

Icarus wouldn't know what the word meant if it hit him in the face, his blue gaze alight with mischief as it tracked a roving Atlas around the room. "Why are you wearing Robin's shirt as a kilt?"

"They fucked," Jenn announced.

The responses were as mixed and hilarious as Robin expected.

Paris, a sighed, "Finally."

Mac, a choked, "What?"

Icarus, a maniacal cackle.

Adam, his head hung.

Abigail, a low whistle.

Mary, clapping from her position at the head of the table.

"Moving on . . ." Robin said with a carry-on gesture.

Only for Atlas to hit replay. "When Robin claimed me yesterday—"

Responses were noticeably less varied, some version of "What the fuck?" echoing around the table—except from Mary.

Of course she knew.

Atlas didn't break his stride, in steps or words, talking over the grenade he'd thrown. "It gave me an idea. The men who snatched me yesterday outside the hunter's house—"

"Wait, back up," Adam said. "We need the full story. Not the fucking one, the kidnapping one."

"Atlas got a text yesterday morning," Robin explained. "It sent him to a house in The Corners."

"The hunter's," Atlas said.

Adam pulled a sheet of paper from his jacket pocket. "That's consistent with what we found." From over his shoulder, Robin studied the regional map—LP to Talahalusi —marked with locations. "Mentions of his appearance over the past few years are concentrated in the South or near reservations. Human, like Atlas said; Indigenous, we think, at least partially so."

"I got a name too," Atlas said. "Cyrus." He held a slip of paper out to Icarus. "Contact info for my excavator. Compare notes."

Icarus opened his laptop, fingers flying, while Mac picked up the interrogation. "Did you find anything there?"

Atlas looked to be heading to the spot beside Robin until Mac's question had him abruptly changing direction. "Nope," he answered, strolling way from Robin. Too casual not to be suspect.

"How'd you know it was his place?" Mac asked.

"They said so."

His answers had become clipped; there was something he didn't want the larger group to know. Robin stepped in before Adam or Mac could press. "It was a setup. Three of Dyami's men jumped him. Took him."

"Took him?" Jenn said. "How'd they manage that?"

"It's possible," Robin said with a sly grin aimed Atlas's direction.

It wasn't enough to lure the warlock back to his side, Atlas posting up across the room from him, back and boot propped against the wall. "I let them. I wanted to get more information."

Probably why he'd stayed out of reach, knowing his motive would piss Robin off. A growl rumbled up from his chest and into his words. "When I intercepted the van, they assumed I was after the bounty on his head."

"Did you know?" Atlas asked him, and Robin nodded. It was a modest contract, not outrageous enough to attract a flood of takers, but high enough to weed out first-timers. Attractive to hunters like Robin, like Cyrus. "Why didn't you take me in? Claim it for yourself?"

"Did you miss that whole key-to-it-all conversation yesterday?"

"That's not—"

Robin cut him off with another truth. "It has never been my intention to give you up."

"Just end me yourself."

That was one solution. But first . . . "After I end your brother."

"Is there a plan in this bickering somewhere?" Mary interrupted.

"We're going to play to Robin's strengths," Atlas said. "To his reputation as a bounty hunter. I can't be the only one Evan has a bounty out on."

"You're not," Robin confirmed.

"And those bounties have other interested parties?"

Robin nodded again.

"Good." He pushed off the wall, roving again. "You're going to steal those bounties out from under him. Get his attention. Then catch me."

"But Evan's seen you two working together," Mac said.

Atlas beat him to the reply, and the vehemence in it surprised Robin, did more funny things to his insides. "Evan's also seen him shunned by all of you, and he's seen us fighting each other. He also knows me."

"What's that supposed to mean?" Icarus said.

"He knows what's at stake if Robin catches me."

"To Mac's point," Abigail said, "doesn't he think Robin caught you already?"

"I didn't take him in and claim the bounty," Robin said, then with a flit of his hand added, "He escaped."

"Not the first time." Atlas landed against the wall next to him with an irritating wink. "Evan will need to see me out in the open. Or at least get reports of it. He also needs to believe the ties here are severed. They're frayed already, so that shouldn't be a stretch."

Seething, Jenn shot off the wall on Robin's other side, and Robin had to throw out an arm to hold her back from murdering his mate. "We don't cut people off like you do."

The murder, however, came from the opposite direction. "Is that so?" Paris's raised voice from across the table drew everyone's attention, indignation unfamiliar in his soft voice, judgment unusual on his typically serene face. "When I found him, when I told him the truth about his sister, he'd been sleeping outside in the field where she died for days."

Jenn immediately retreated, gaze cast aside as she tucked her tail and slunk to Abigail's side.

Rotating on his shoulder, Atlas angled Robin's direction, and when he spoke, it was a request, not an order. For Robin's decision, irrespective of the opinion of anyone else in the room. "There needs to be another visible blowup, in case anyone is watching. Can you do it?"

His call, his will, his independence. "I can do it."

TWENTY-FOUR

It had been a decade since Robin set foot in his childhood home. Not much had changed inside since and yet his entire world outside it had been turned upside down.

The family home—a two-story stucco structure built into the side of a hill, halfway up the mountain Mac's mother's people referred to as Kanamota—was well cared for. Freshly painted a soft white, none of the roof's terracotta tiles missing, the windows sparkling clean. The home cared well for its inhabitants too, its location naturally protected from elements and enemies, its foundations strong and sturdy, surviving the earth's shifts for three generations of Whelans.

From the main floor balcony where Robin stood, the grounds around the home seemed similarly in order. Among the cultivated fields that dotted the forest clearings, half of them were beginning to show the first shoots of winter vegetables, while the other half were at rest until spring when they'd be planted with sunflowers, sage, and more.

And beyond the homestead, the peaks and valleys of the pack's range were just beginning to recover from the long hot summer. In a couple rainy months' time, the peaks would be green and the valley floor awash with yellow from the wild mustard that flourished in these parts.

Growing up, March had always been his favorite time to run, when the towering, swaying weeds made the range feel a little less huge. When the mustard reminded him of his mother. They'd laid him and his sister on her chest right after their birth, as she'd struggled for breath, the life bleeding out of her, and she'd smelled like the wild mustard did under his paws.

"Never thought I'd see you back here."

Robin rotated away from the view to the older man standing over the balcony threshold. "Uncle."

Jasper's strawberry blond hair was thinner and streaked with more white than the last time Robin had seen him, but those white hairs and the deeper wrinkles around his eyes and mouth were the only signs of age on his mother's brother, the man who'd raised him and Deborah.

Their father had died within a year of their mother. A broken heart, everyone had said. A self-inflicted gunshot wound, the police report said. Jasper had seen Robin through that and more, until the day of Deborah's funeral when he'd told Robin that he never wanted to see him again.

Toned arms folded, Jasper's stature was as imposing as Robin remembered, his golden eyes as sharp and discerning as they'd been whenever Robin had pulled explosion-worthy stunts as a teen. "What brings the prodigal son home?"

"I need Mom's letters." There'd been a stack of them

waiting for him and Deborah when they'd come of age. Everything she'd wanted them to know in case she didn't survive their birth, like she'd somehow known she wouldn't. He'd read them countless times over, looking for clues and finding few, the mate bit having stuck with—frightened—him most. Now, given that the mate bit had come true, and given everything else he'd learned the past few months, plus the wealth of knowledge in said mate's head, he might connect the dots he hadn't recognized before.

"They're gone," Jasper said, as he wandered back into the great room.

Robin followed, momentarily distracted by the additional pack members who'd gathered inside, including Jenn and Abigail. Their wide-eyed expressions indicated they were just as surprised as him by Jenn's father's statement.

"Gone where?" Robin asked, trying to squash the tangle of anger and panic rising in his voice. No way Jasper would destroy those; they were all he had left of his sister. They were all Robin had left of his mother. After he'd last read them, the day of Deborah's funeral, he'd put them into the family safe like he and Deborah had always done. Jenn, who'd assumed the mantle of pack leader after Deborah's death, had assured him they'd always be there, as part of the pack's historical record.

"I burned them."

Jenn vaulted off the arm of the couch. "Why'd you do that?"

"In case this war you two"—Jasper waggled a finger between them—"are set on fighting goes the other way."

"You'd fold?" Robin scoffed. "Just like that?"

"I'm protecting our family and this pack."

Robin glanced around the room, meeting each pack member's gaze. "Do all of you feel that way?"

"We're with Jenn," said Bruce, her younger brother.

"And I'm with her, always," Jenn replied, her devotion to Nature unwavering, but when she swung her gaze to Robin, it was clear her feelings toward him were more than just an act's worth. "But where are you, cousin?"

"What's that supposed to mean?"

"You turned Paris over to a giant," Abigail said, and Robin's gaze shot to the most level-headed member of their team, the one who understood nuance better than most, abandoned by a pack who had allied themselves with a giant.

"Just like your mate did," Jenn added.

"I didn't know he was my mate, then," he barked back.

It was a risky move, bringing Atlas into this. Volatile for their pack, and if someone was leaking information to Evan, how would this change the calculus? Would he believe that Atlas, once he caught Robin, would ever turn his mate over? Was Jenn even considering that or just acting out of frustration and anger?

Regardless, the cat was out of the bag. "Wait?" Bruce said. "The same warlock who killed Deborah?"

"He didn't," Robin corrected. "It was his twin."

"Because that's so much better," another of their cousins, Olivia, said from where she'd been eyeing something out the window.

"You vanish for days on end, Robin," Jenn said, drawing his attention back to her. "You don't let anyone in on your plans." She swallowed hard. "You don't answer pack calls."

His gut roiled, familiar guilt creeping up his throat, his

voice rough with it as he gritted out his response. "I have answered every one of them the past two months."

"How much of the past two months," Jasper said, "could have been avoided if you'd answered the call ten years ago?"

And as fast as the guilt had climbed, it brought him low, taking his stomach to the floor, same as it always did when the worst mistake of his life was thrown back in his face. "So, we're back to that?"

"Once a traitor, always a traitor."

Good to know where he stood. While this may have started as an act, the performance had been hijacked by the truth, which made what he came here for all the more important. He'd never get another chance. "Give me Mom's letters."

"I told you—"

"Give them to me," Robin roared, the voice he would have used to give an order if he'd taken control of the pack after Deborah. By birthright, he'd deserved it; by deed, he'd forfeited it. Instincts were instincts, though, and everyone but Jasper took a step back and lowered their heads.

While he didn't join them in physically submitting, Jasper tempered his voice, the tone deferential, when he spoke again. "She was my sister."

"She was my mother," Robin said, letting every bit of sorrow bleed into his words. "You had a lifetime with her. I had minutes. If you don't want anything to do with me, fine. But give me that piece of her, of my history, and I'll never show my face here again."

Jenn gasped. "Robin—"

He kept his gaze locked on his uncle. "Do we have a deal?"

The older man stared him down another long minute before seeming to accept the truth of Robin's words and nodding to Bruce, who disappeared into the house.

"Robin." Jenn stepped to his side, hand on his forearm, tears glistening in her eyes. "You don't have to do this."

He covered her hand, giving it a squeeze, as he forced out words around the lump in his throat. She was a good pack leader; she didn't need the albatross that was him hanging around her neck. "I do, cuz."

Bruce returned with the stack of letters, tied together by the green and yellow ribbons of Robin's memories. He handed them to Jasper, who slapped them into Robin's outstretched hand. "Willow deserved better. So did Deborah."

Robin didn't disagree.

TWENTY-FIVE

Near the end of the half-mile gravel drive, Robin reached for the hem of his shirt to undress before shifting when Atlas stepped out of the woods. "That should do the trick."

"You were there?"

"Close enough to hear the good bits."

Robin's answering laugh sounded as cold as his insides felt.

"Come this way," Atlas said with a tip of his head toward the woods he'd just appeared out of.

A few minutes later, once the replays in Robin's head quieted enough to appreciate reality's comfortable silence, he realized where they were headed. Following Atlas, he didn't bother to hide his smile, grateful for it to chase away the chill. "I used to come here as a kid," he said, as they emerged from the trees beside a small reservoir pond. Surrounded by tall pines, the little lake had always felt like an oasis amid the vastness.

"Damn." Atlas clicked his tongue against the back of his

teeth. "I was hoping to surprise you." His rolling eyes belied his words. "Maybe this will do?" he added, as he pulled out a joint.

"That'll do," Robin said. "Could use a smoke."

Atlas lit the joint with a flick of fire from his fingertip and handed it to Robin. A few puffs to get it going, then he inhaled a lungful of earthy peace before passing the joint back. He wandered out onto the short wooden dock where he and Deborah used to spend countless hours as kids, daydreaming about all the places they were going to visit one day. She'd done it as a soldier, then a federal agent; he'd done it as a tracker.

Hunting was always hardest when it was someone close to you. He shucked out of his flannel, wrapped his mother's letters in the fabric, then lowered himself onto the dock beside Atlas. "You think someone in the pack is a traitor."

"Statistically speaking, yes." He handed the joint back, then reclined on the dock, his eyes closed, the setting sun painting his blond hair and pale skin in shades of orange and violet. Everyone always talked about how pretty Paris was, and the Cirillo heir admittedly had runway model good looks. By contrast, Atlas, in suits or kilts, had an untouchable ethereal quality to his appearance that was hilariously at odds with every other acerbic side of him. "I'm sorry."

Not acerbic, and not the sentiment out of Atlas's mouth that Robin needed. The last thing he wanted was Atlas's pity. "Don't," he told him. "This is already weird as fuck."

Atlas's sexy, smart-ass laugh was more like it, and Robin caught on to the trap he'd walked into. "You did that on purpose, didn't you?"

Atlas rotated on his side toward him, dancing green eyes glancing up at him. "Worked, didn't it?" Then down to the mound of flannel and parchment between them. "What are those?"

"Letters from my mother, to me and Deborah."

"What do you hope to find in them?"

"Answers. Things I thought were cryptic before are starting to connect now. I need to reread them. You need to read them. See if there's something we can use."

Atlas righted himself, and Robin anticipated an argument over *we* just to make him feel better. Instead, Atlas dug out his phone, tapped the screen a few times, then held the device out to him. "You need to read this first."

He traded him the joint for the phone and read the posted contract. "This is the bounty you want to go after?"

"Not me, her. She thinks he's hiding a phoenix."

"Which is why Evan would want him too. But if I catch him, turn him over to the team, then all that"—he gestured back to the house—"was for naught."

He shook his head. "She just wants a meet. An alliance for when the time comes."

Robin continued reading. "This says he'll be at Club Sutro tonight."

Atlas finished the joint and snuffed it out on the dock. "We'll need to leave enough time to swing by the condo and distillery."

Leave enough, as in they didn't have to leave right away. They had time for something else. And by the blush that hit Atlas's cheeks, the warlock was thinking about the same something else as Robin. Something that would make them both feel better. Robin laid Atlas's phone atop the letters and pushed them well out of the way. "We have some time until then."

Green eyes, the color of the forest around them, heated from more than just the sun reflecting off the water. "What do you have in mind?"

Closing the distance between them, Robin propped one hand behind Atlas's back and snuck the other through the gap in his makeshift kilt, skirting his fingers over his inner thigh. "You remember what I said about the next time I fucked you?"

"Yes, but . . ." Atlas's words stuttered on a moan when Robin nuzzled behind his ear, a full body shiver rippling through him. Robin's own cock hardened, Atlas's reaction, plus the waft of his scent that tickled Robin's nose, a potent combination. Atlas found his words again, but they were breathy, uttered on a gasp as Robin trailed his hand higher. "That was ten—eleven?—fucks ago now."

The backs of his knuckles brushed his cock, his lips the shell of Atlas's ear. "Yes, but you weren't wearing a kilt then."

"I'm still not," he snapped, haughty making a come-back. Always a last line of defense, their perfect foreplay. "I'm wearing your shirt."

Robin grinned, this entire encounter, the push and pull where they both won, exactly what he needed. He adjusted his hand, fingers curling around Atlas's length and giving him a long, slow tug, his thumb circling the damp tip when he reached it. "Might be even sexier."

He was so distracted by the rising color on Atlas's cheeks, by his darkening eyes, by the rock-hard cock in his hand, that Robin missed Atlas moving his own until he closed it over his erection, palming him through his jeans.

"When you fuck me with this fat cock like you promised, I want to enjoy it. I don't want to be on the clock, and I don't want to be in the fucking woods."

Robin rocked up to meet the rough handling, loving every aggressive second of it. Then rocked his entire body closer, withdrawing his hand from between Atlas's thighs and dragging his thumb over Atlas's bottom lip, smearing it with his own precome. "Sometimes the truth does come out of this mouth."

"Too often lately."

Like it had just then, but Robin was too turned on to call him on it, and the last thing he wanted to do was derail where this heated teasing was headed, the truth their bodies were seeking. "I know how to stop that, for now."

"How's that?" Atlas replied coyly, then proving he already knew the answer, sucked Robin's thumb into his mouth, swirling his tongue around the tip like Robin's finger had him, like he was making sure to lick up every drop of precome Robin had collected.

Too much, too good, not enough. "Stretch that pretty mouth around my cock."

"Will that make you forget about it?"

Another slip, a truth offered in return. "For a little while."

Their gazes locked, truths and sorrows acknowledged, commiseration accepted, before Atlas flipped open the shirt-kilt, took his cock in hand, and continued to jerk himself. Robin wasted no time unfastening his jeans and getting his own cock out, the cool air barely grazing his overheated skin before it was enveloped in scorching heat, Atlas's mouth closing around him while he continued to stroke himself.

Pleasuring them both.

Robin threaded his fingers through Atlas's thick blond waves, held on tight, and forgot about everything but the heat flooding his senses, the whisper of spring chasing away the chill he hadn't escaped in far too long.

TWENTY-SIX

It felt good to work again, even if Robin did always feel out of place at Club Sutro.

Jeans, flannel, and hair that hadn't seen a proper cut in years didn't exactly fit the mold of Yerba Buena's most exclusive club. This was more Icarus's scene, alluring courtesans winding through the crowd of wealthy patrons. It had been Paris's too, before he'd settled down, heirs like him nursing high-end booze from crystal glassware that somehow survived the thumping music. And before Paris was even old enough to frequent clubs, Sutro had been Deb's scene, a place for her to let off steam and dance with her husbands after dealing with pack business and work trips.

"You want another beer?"

Kai's question knocked Robin out of the past and back to the present. He glanced over his shoulder at Paris's other best friend, Jason's raven partner, who was working the bar tonight. Robin traded his empty for the fresh bottle Kai offered. "Thanks."

The raven disappeared to the opposite end of the bar, waiting on another customer, and Robin turned his attention back to the packed club. One would never guess that two months ago a giant had come crashing through the ceiling, the furniture and walls had been riddled with bullet holes, and a certain blond warlock had stood atop the backbar and fired a crossbow bolt into another giant.

Tonight, Robin was hunting a different blond: Glen Brewster, a six-foot-two bear shifter who led a loosely affiliated group of his kind that inhabited the coastal woods north of YB. And Robin wasn't the only one on the hunt for Mr. Brewster. In one of the large booths by the windows, a feline shifter of some sort was trying and failing to fit in with the other patrons in his booth who were drinking and laughing merrily. And on the dance floor, a pair of humans were getting all kinds of attention as they put on an amorous couple looking for a third routine, inviting others to dance with them. A clever trap for Glen, if he ever showed.

Robin was beginning to doubt he would when finally the bear shifter strode through the door—with a big beefy arm looped around Atlas's waist.

Not the plan.

So not the plan.

Atlas was on perimeter duty. He was supposed to radio when Glen was close, then stay outside, in case things inside went sideways and Robin needed an emergency escape snap while dashing out.

He was *not* supposed to let another man put his hands on him.

The only thing that kept Robin from vaulting off his barstool was the fact Atlas wasn't pretending to be Evan.

He was very much in his Atlas element, blond hair perfectly coiffed, chin held high, wearing the kilt and leather harness he'd changed into at his condo.

Evan needed to see—or at least hear about—his twin being free and out in the open, no longer Robin's prisoner. And there he was, on the dance floor at Club Sutro in another man's arms. Two flashing neon targets for the three other bounty hunters in the room. "Shit."

Jason squeezed in next to him at the bar. "There was an altercation outside," he whispered low. The phoenix had already been at the club when Robin arrived, and because Robin still didn't fully trust his mate, he'd roped Jason into reconning the recon man.

"Who?" Robin asked.

"Another bounty hunter. We dispatched him. Glen was going to leave, but Atlas convinced him to come inside and forget about it."

Forget about it.

Robin clenched his teeth. Was that what Atlas said to all the guys? Had he just been giving him the same line earlier at the lake?

"What do you want to do here?" Jason asked as he raked a hand through his dark unruly curls.

"Kill him."

"Yes, we all know. But like, right now, what do you want to do?"

Robin jutted his chin toward the hunter in the booth. "The feline shifter on the end there is here for the same reason as us. Get Kai to give you a bottle of bourbon on Adam's tab, then go join them. Box the shifter in."

"What are you going to do?" Jason asked.

"See the flirty human couple on the dance floor?"

"The ones looking for a third?"

Robin nodded. "More like hunters looking to lure their target. I'm going to make sure neither Atlas nor Glen end up in their hands."

"On it," Jason said, then wove his way to the other end of the bar, leaning over it to whisper in his boyfriend's ear.

With the feline shifter handled, Robin focused on his targets and enacted a plan to foil theirs. He tipped back the rest of his beer, slid off the stool, and removed his flannel, stripping down to the black tank he had on underneath.

Heads swiveled his direction, including a certain blond one, the owner's green gaze furious.

Good.

Even better that the bounty hunter pair had also picked him up on his way to the dance floor. He hadn't danced in years, but he must have been convincing enough, the woman hunter crooking her finger to call him over. Robin's gaze slid back to Atlas, who was watching him over Glen's shoulder, the bear shifter oblivious to his partner's wandering eye. Robin made a deliberate sweep of his gaze, to the booth where Jason was sliding in next to the hunter there, then back to the couple who had eyes on him. Identifying the threats for Atlas before Robin returned his attention to the couple meeting him halfway on the dance floor.

The woman slung an arm over his shoulder, drawing him closer while her partner hemmed him in from behind, his tall, toned body pressed against Robin's back. "How about we make a deal?" the woman said. "The three of us take the two of them." She tipped her head toward where Atlas and Glen were dancing. "Then we split the bounties three ways?"

"I don't need your help," Robin said.

The sharp point of a blade pressed against his back, right over his kidney. "We don't need you either," the man said. "Call it professional courtesy."

"You think you can catch them?" Robin replied. "A warlock who can snap his way out of anywhere and a giant bear shifter."

"The warlock got away from you," the woman said. "You need us too."

Robin pretended to be conflicted while swaying between the bodies on either side of him.

"What'll it be?" the guy said, and Robin honestly wondered if he was asking about the bounties or the boner he notched against the seam of Robin's jeans, sliding it along his ass crack.

"All right," Robin said, playing along and rocking back his hips, distracting the already distracted. "You two take the warlock. He's smaller. I'll take the shifter."

He didn't give them a chance to argue, ducking out from between them and spinning toward Atlas and Glen. The head start gave him time to crowd behind Glen and whisper, "Did he explain to you what's going on?"

"I'm in," the bear said.

"Good, then shift!"

A giant bear appearing in the middle of a crowded club was a recipe for disaster. Add a roaring coyote and a warlock throwing orbs of green magic, and almost everyone was headed to the exits. None of the other paranormals, including Jason's mark, wanted any part of the chaos.

Only the two human hunters were dumb enough to try and battle Atlas while Robin made a show of cornering the bear. He lunged, no teeth, and Glen made it seem like he was surrendering, letting Robin hold him down by the neck. If word got back to Evan, it would be of a catch by Robin. And of another escape by his twin, Atlas using his magic to throw the hunter pair into the backbar before snapping out of there.

TWENTY-SEVEN

It was near dawn by the time everyone else cleared out of the distillery tasting room, alliances made and another phoenix in Mary's pocket.

Robin didn't care about any of that. All he cared about was setting the record straight with the warlock in a kilt sprawled on the chaise. Turning his back on the reckless fucker, he busied himself with a shot of vodka to avoid charging across the room and wringing Atlas's neck. "You want to tell me what the fuck that was?"

"*That* was a successful operation."

"*That* wasn't the plan."

"I improvised."

The absolute arrogance was enraging, the growl bleeding into his voice. "Without a word of warning."

"I told you, I don't—"

Robin slammed his glass down and rounded on him, unleashing a roared warning. "Don't you fucking say it."

Atlas's smirk would be the death of him. The warlock rose from the couch and sauntered across the room. "Don't tell me you didn't love it. Thinking on your feet, setting traps, negotiating a deal in two seconds flat."

Robin met him halfway, beside the table Atlas had leaned a hip against. "I didn't love seeing another man's hands on my mate."

Atlas's eyes flared, as if he didn't expect Robin to put the word to their connection. But then his mossy irises turned a darker shade of green, like the forest just before a summer storm, like maybe *mate* wasn't a bad thing at all. He pushed off the table, narrowing the space between them, and when he spoke, voice dangerously low, the snap of his order—"Take the flannel off"—went straight to Robin's dick. "And the undershirt."

He didn't hesitate to pull them both off over his head, even as part of him railed at how fast Atlas had turned the tables. A bigger part of him didn't give a damn, loved it even. Loved Atlas's hands on him too, the warlock gliding them up his front as he pressed close behind him. "I didn't love seeing another man's dick rutting against what's mine either. Or you rutting back."

"I was improvising," Robin said, parroting Atlas's words, then lifting his ass to rut against his mate's cock.

Atlas clasped his hip, holding him close as he rolled back. "I didn't need to know you could dance."

"I was rusty."

He nipped the back of his shoulder. "You were sexy as hell, and no one in that club could take their eyes off you."

Robin glanced over his shoulder. "Including you?"

"Including me." Atlas lifted his gaze, and the pure heat staring up at Robin was the final straw.

Using his speed, he spun and shoved Atlas against the nearest post, crowding into his space, gripping his face the way he liked and forcing that burning green gaze back to his. Atlas needed to understand the tightrope he was walking, the razor-thin patience he was playing with. "If you'd come in there in a suit, I might have killed you."

"He needed—"

"To know you were free, I got that."

"And I needed to make sure you kept your promise." He lifted a hand and snapped, leaving Robin with a handful of green mist and a gut full of boiling anger.

But only for a split second.

The sneaky bastard reappeared on the table, his legs spread and that devastating smirk back in place. "Starting with sucking my cock."

Bare, underneath the kilt he flipped up.

His erection was as stiff as Robin's, the head glistening with a bead of precome that Robin descended on. Atlas's cock wasn't as fat or as long as his, but it was perfectly proportioned to his compact frame and perfectly sized for Robin's mouth. He could swirl his tongue around it on each pull to the tip, stretch his mouth all the way around it's girth as he descended to the root again, his nose buried in the wiry hairs there, Atlas's real scent intoxicating.

He'd happily spend all day there, Atlas's cock in his mouth, his nose buried in the first breaths of spring, but the horny warlock had other ideas, his fingers curling in his hair, nails scraping across his scalp. "Fucking suck me off like you mean it."

For that sass, he got a slap to his thigh and the rough working over he obviously wanted, Robin sliding his hands under his buttocks, using them for leverage, then setting a relentless pace. Fast hard sucks that made Atlas groan, flicks of his tongue under the head that made him curse, the hint of teeth that made him hiss, Robin's fingers digging into his ass cheeks, then sliding into his crack, making him shout for more. Robin kept him right there on the edge of pleasure and torture.

Half reclined, Atlas's bare chest strained against the leather harness as he white-knuckled the edge of the table, holding on for dear life. "Now, you maddening coyote, fucking now."

Given the swell of his own cock still trapped in his jeans, Robin finally conceded, ready to claim the hole he'd been teasing just as mercilessly. A couple fast flicks under the head, then he closed his lips around Atlas's cock again, took it all the way to the back of his throat, and growled.

Atlas exploded with a shout, filling Robin's mouth with come. He swallowed some and held the rest in reserve. To do what he'd promised. Straightening, he flipped Atlas over on the table, nothing gentle about it, spread his ass cheeks, nothing gentle there either, and opened his mouth, forcing Atlas's own come into his hole with his tongue.

"Fuck," Atlas keened, slapping a hand on the table. "Please, please, please."

Robin didn't think he'd ever heard anything as sweet as a blissed-out Atlas Shaw begging.

He begged even louder once Robin shoved his cock in that come-slick hole. For "more," for "harder," for Robin to "please, come" so he'd get his tongue back on him. Gripping the harness for leverage, Robin rammed into him as hard and as fast as his body allowed.

He didn't last long after that, the sight of a writhing, sweaty Atlas, the promise of the scent of them together on his tongue too intoxicating, too erotic to withstand, his climax rushing up and claiming him like the man below him.

And as he buried his face back between Atlas's pale, round ass cheeks, his tongue swiping over his messy, quivering hole, he realized his imagination had nothing on the real thing.

This was spring, summer, fall, and winter all wrapped into one.

He'd never been more certain this man was his mate, that he'd do anything to keep him for as long as they had on this earth.

TWENTY-EIGHT

"Did you think we wouldn't find it?"

Atlas ignored Adam's question and boosted himself onto the table where Robin had done all manner of filthy things to him yesterday. They'd gone their separate ways later that morning, each of them needing to be seen in public without the other to dispel any rumors that they'd been working together at Club Sutro. Robin had spent nearly every second of the past thirty-six hours mentally replaying Atlas's shouts and groans, remembering the silky hardness of his cock and the tight heat of his hole, fantasizing about when he'd get to taste and smell him again.

Atlas's gaze drifted to where Robin stood behind the bar and one corner of his mouth hitched up, as if he knew exactly where Robin's mind had drifted. He hadn't jerked off once since they'd parted, and he was paying for it now. Atlas wasn't helping, dressed in another tight tee and kilt, the tartan riding high on his thighs. Robin flipped him the bird and the other side of the sexy fucker's mouth turned up in a sly grin.

He was so distracted he missed Icarus hurling a balled-up napkin at him, hitting him square in the forehead. "Do you mind?"

"You two called this meeting," Robin said with a shrug. "I can't help that you put us in the same room together after a day apart. And for the record, you two are just as bad."

Icarus glanced over his shoulder at his partner. "That's true."

Adam rolled his eyes, then tossed the first of the four folders under his arm onto the other table in the middle of the room, photos scattering across the tabletop. "There's a wall of pictures in the hunter's house. Of Atlas and his family."

Fantasies forgotten, Robin shot out from behind the bar to get a better look at reality. No, not reality, a nightmare. It was a massive collage—pictures of Atlas, of his brothers, of an older man he assumed was Atlas's father, based on resemblance. Some of the photos were posed, some were surveillance, taken from afar and up close, taken as recently as Atlas's brother's funeral.

He whipped his gaze to the liar still sitting on the table. "You didn't think I needed to know about this?" Atlas had told him he'd found nothing at Cyrus's house.

"Not until I knew more."

"That's not how this works."

He hopped off the table. "That's how this has always worked."

The detachment in his words, in the tilt of his chin and the coolness of gaze, was a one-eighty from the flirty Atlas of seconds ago. Robin felt the whiplash in his chest and his balls.

"What else did you find out?" Atlas asked Adam.

"His mother was Indigenous, Bay Miwok, and the original owner of the house." He tossed a second folder onto the table, this one a mix of papers and photo. "Malila Contra."

Tan skin, short dark hair, dark eyes, tall and imposing. Robin could see where her son got his height from.

"Lila?"

Robin jerked his gaze up, not used to hearing Atlas's voice so strangled. He'd only ever heard it like that when Atlas was about to come, when his gaze was lust-clouded and his cheeks rosy. Right then, Atlas's eyes were wide with surprise and his face was pale.

He looked like he'd seen a ghost.

The ex-cop was no stranger to that look. "You knew her?" Adam asked.

"Knew," Robin said, picking up on the past tense. Same as Adam's earlier *was*. "She's dead?"

Icarus waved a hand over the pile of Shaw family pictures. "See giant wall of vengeance."

Atlas didn't take the bait, a rarity where Icarus's softballs were concerned. He wandered over to the bar instead, grabbed the bottle of vodka, and tipped it up to his lips, not bothering with a glass. Two big gulps later, he lowered the bottle and wiped his mouth with the back of his hand. "She was the human who held Chaos before it was cast to the other side of the veil."

"She was also your father's mistress," Adam said, dropping the third folder, open to a birth certificate. For Cyrus Contra. Malila Contra was listed as mother; Pierce Shaw as father. "That"—he tapped the grainy photo on the other side of the folder, Malila holding a baby, seemingly in an argument with Atlas's father—"is your half brother."

"I can't believe you used your father's name as an alias," Icarus said to Atlas.

Atlas strode to the table and mimicked Icarus's earlier gesture, hand circling over the collage of his father. "See giant wall of asshole. It fit."

"I was so robbed of a punch."

"Why is Cyrus trying to kill you?" Adam asked, righting the conversation.

"Has he actually tried to kill you?" Robin queried instead, this latest information putting a new spin on Cyrus's prior appearance. "Or is it possible he just wants to have a conversation?"

Atlas glared at him. "I know what someone looks like when they want to kill me. He does."

"What's he after, then?" Adam said. "Your father's approval?"

"Maybe," Icarus replied. "His asshole dad does hate him."

Robin couldn't make any of those deductions without more context. "When did Lila die?"

"A few years after the Rift," Adam replied.

Almost there. "How?" he asked Atlas, sensing the truth would blow things wide open.

Sure enough. "My mother and Daphne's cast Chaos behind the veil again. Lila didn't survive the spell."

Wall of vengeance was right, from multiple angles. "And he's been after your family ever since?"

"Apparently."

Robin shifted into tactical mode, requiring a plan to protect his mate. "Do we have a location on him?"

Beneath Cyrus's birth certificate was a map of Yerba Buena, dotted with red X marks, a cluster of them in the

Lost Valley. "Sightings over the past three days," Adam said.

"Fucking hell," Robin cursed. "This place is burned."

Icarus groaned. "We're going to have to move all that shit again."

Robin ignored his whining, more concerned with their safety. "Get back to the mountain," he told Adam and Icarus. "Fill them in." Then to Atlas, said, "Go to the condo. No one can get past those spells."

As if the barked order had brought him back to life, Atlas straightened his spine and lifted his chin, barking back. "I'm not going to fucking hide. We're six days from Solstice. We need to keep luring Evan out."

"On that note . . ." Adam handed Robin the final file. "You look like you could kill someone."

"Please."

Robin flipped open the folder. On one side was a dossier for a witch who'd previously been a member of the Redwood Coven. On the other side was her photo. Attractive, middle-aged, white, with blue eyes, light brown hair, and a button nose.

"Your other brother," Adam said, "just doubled the bounty on this witch."

"What's she to Evan?" Robin asked.

"A potential rival. Mac talked to his contacts in the coven. They tossed her out decades ago when they learned she was working against them to bring Chaos through the veil."

And there went the color in Atlas's face again, but he didn't shrink like he had before. Almost like he knew the answer to this mystery and was steeling himself for it. "Name?"

"Karoline Wiles," Robin read from the dossier.

His eyes slipped closed, but not before Robin recognized the guilt that streaked through his green gaze. "She's one of Chaos's devotees."

"What else?"

"She was the one who recruited me, who tempted me with the promise of Chaos for a while."

Robin saw red, imagining the worst of what all that entailed for Atlas, understanding that glimpse of guilt now, better than most. He felt it too, every time he killed, every time he remembered the day he let his sister get killed too.

"It's a trap," Atlas's words yanked him out of the familiar mire. "Evan could easily defeat her. He did defeat her already. He doesn't need to hire the job out, and he certainly doesn't need to double the bounty."

"So he wants us on her," Robin said, following the train of thought, recalling what Atlas had previously said—he knew Evan better than anyone, and vice versa, even if Robin intended to change that eventually. "While he does what?"

"Eliminates the real threat to Chaos—Pati Miwra's son."

TWENTY-NINE

Robin checked his phone for the umpteenth time over the past six hours. No word from the team at Monte Corvo, no word from the pack, no word from Atlas. He hadn't seen any of them for two days, only communicating via encrypted texts. The team had been moving Pati and Pax, Atlas had been investigating Cyrus and working with Mary to prepare for Solstice, and Robin had been hunting Karoline.

Which was how he'd ended up in the Canyon Lands, Yerba Buena's mystical equivalent of a terror-filled funhouse. Nature had conceded this area of YB during the Rift, the weather magically and naturally terrible, the land unstable, more of it falling into the Bay each day, and the carcasses of once-gleaming buildings reduced to rubble.

Robin found himself crouched in one of those broken buildings, peering through sheets of rain, ears attuned, for any sign of Karoline at the meet that was supposed to take place in the building across the crumbled street below.

He checked his phone again.

"They'll call if they need you."

He whipped around with a growl. Not because he felt threatened—he'd know that voice anywhere—but because the asshole was playing with fire, sneaking around when Robin was already on edge. When he hadn't smelled him, touched him, kissed him in two fucking days.

"Not nice, is it?" Atlas said, strolling toward him. "Someone sneaking up on you without making a sound." He flicked his fingers. "Covering their scent."

Robin didn't inhale too deeply, certain he'd jump the man with the slightest provocation. He lightly sniffed the air, just enough Atlas to settle the queasiness that had swished around in his belly since they'd parted. "You started it." He rotated back around, peering once more through the rain for any movement in the empty room across the street. Still dark, still quiet. He sank to his ass and relaxed back against the frame of the long-gone plate glass window. "And you shouldn't be here either," he said to Atlas.

He wisely lowered himself across from Robin and rested back against the opposite side of the window frame, only their feet in touching distance. "I'm here in case you get the call. You can't be in two places at once."

And fuck if Robin didn't want to crawl on his hands and knees across the floor and kiss the fuck out of the man, the enemy turned mate, who somehow seemed to understand him best.

He'd like to understand him better too so he could return the care and concern. "Why didn't you tell me about the wall at Cyrus's place?"

His gaze drifted outside, but by the faraway look in his green eyes, Atlas was somewhere—sometime—else completely. "*We* doesn't end well for folks around me," he said. "Cole, Daphne, Canton, Paris. The last thing I wanted was for my shit, another person targeting me and mine, to also target you and yours."

Except Atlas was his now, and he was Atlas's. Those lines of separation were getting blurrier every day.

"And Karoline? You're not just here in case I get the call, are you?"

"I intended to take care of things myself."

Robin knocked his foot, once, twice, until Atlas gave him his attention. "What if it's a double blind? I leave, Evan shows up instead of Karoline, and you've got no backup."

He shrugged. "Then he takes me, and you come to the rescue."

"If he doesn't kill you first."

"Last," he said, barely a whisper, and the guilt he didn't bother to hide this time made Robin's chest ache. Fuck, it was like looking in a mirror. He rested his foot against Atlas's. "I know what it feels like."

Atlas pressed back with his. "I know you do."

They stayed that way, in each other's quiet company, as the rain outside turned to a mist and the building across the street remained dark, the only movement in the vicinity the ground periodically shifting beneath them. "I hate it here," Atlas grumbled.

"It's not so bad," Robin said. He wished he'd had a camera ready to capture Atlas's aghast expression. "The ruins and fence keep it all contained and when the fog's in, it's like a blanket."

"Yeah," Atlas scoffed. "A cold, wet one."

Robin chuckled. "It's not so overwhelming here, and in

a fight, it's close work, hand to hand combat, no fancy devices, just pure skill."

"And obstacles, like not being able to see a foot in front of you."

"You were here all the time for Vincent."

"I know, and I hated it."

Since Atlas seemed to be feeling truthful, Robin asked another question that had been weighing on his mind. "Your time with Karoline and Lila . . . Is that how you convinced Vincent to trust you? That you were on the same side?"

"A man like Vincent hears and sees what he wants to." He nodded at the dark, empty space across the street. "Same as her."

It was Robin's turn to gasp. "I thought she recruited you?"

"Yes, but I went in as a spy first."

"What changed?"

"I got tired, same as you, of being a pawn. She promised me freedom, independence. But if she, Evan, and Chaos get what they want—"

"There'll be no place left worth being free in."

A light flickered on across the street, Karoline entered the room, and for one terrifying, heart-stopping second, Robin thought he'd lost him, Atlas snapping right out from in front of him.

But a single beat of Robin's heart later, Atlas appeared behind him, hidden in the shadows, out of the moonlight that had broken through the clouds and shown exactly where he'd been standing.

"Fuck," Robin cursed.

Atlas clasped the outsides of his shoulders. "I needed to act fast. And so do you. You need to get to the pack."

Robin spun to face him. "What? I haven't—" The phone in his pocket buzzed.

"You need to go."

He glanced over his shoulder. Still just Karoline in the room. "Atlas . . ."

"Hey," he said softly, and just as gently grasped his chin and used it to draw his attention back to him. "She won't hurt me."

Except for the hit his soul would take when he had to kill again, like it had when he'd killed Daphne. But if Daphne hadn't known about Mary, Robin was sure now that Atlas would have . . . "You're going to give her a chance to change her mind, aren't you?"

He pressed his lips together.

And Robin jumped to the next logical conclusion. "Same as you're going to give your brother."

He slid the hand on his jaw higher, cupping his cheek. "I promise, you will still get what you deserve." Robin wanted to argue but the phone in his pocket buzzed again. Atlas firmed the grip on his face. "Go."

Robin returned the hold and drew Atlas closer, nose to nose, growling a "Yours" against his lips.

Atlas's "Mine" bled into a kiss that was wild and peaceful all at once, that made Robin's soul settle in that certain way his mother had talked about in her letters. Like Mac must have found with Paris, like Adam with Icarus, and before that with David and Deborah, like his and Deb's mother had shared with their father.

Like maybe he'd found freedom.

THIRTY

Each mile closer to the pack homestead made Robin more uneasy.

Not because he'd left his mate in the Canyon Lands. Atlas could take care of himself. The warlock had made it fuck-all-knew how long before their paths had crossed.

And not because Robin was breaking a promise returning here. Jenn had called; he answered.

And not even because Jenn had needed to call him; crisis at this point was inevitable.

No, it wasn't anything so monumental, more a sense of absence he couldn't put his finger on, a chill crawling up his spine, a smell that was unmistakable as he neared the lake where he and Atlas had shared a joint and gotten off together a few days ago.

Unlike then, it was the middle of the night, pitch black outside, the trees still dripping from the earlier rain. And someone was dead in these woods.

He wasn't surprised when a violet-eyed Liam sailed overhead, croaking a mournful *Kraa*. He circled once more, another *Kraa* to alert Jenn, Jason, and Abigail to his presence. A quick change of clothes later, Robin emerged from the woods to join them.

"Pati or one of the team?" he asked his cousin. Jenn wouldn't have called him here for just any dead pack member; he'd missed plenty of those over the years. This one had to involve one of their team or Pati and Pax, who were being moved between safe houses daily.

"Pati," she answered. "Still alive, we think, but her escorts…" She ran a hand over her head, growling when she met her ponytail holder. "They were taking her and Pax to the handoff spot." Her voice was rough, her eyes bloodshot and puffy. "Fuck, I should have gone with them."

"Liam and I were supposed to meet them," Jason said, then cast his gaze aside. "Paris met them first. He called us, and I called Jenn."

They. Multiple souls who'd contacted the medium. Multiple deaths.

"How long ago?"

"Two hours."

"And you just called me?" he barked, frustration turning up the volume of his voice. Unjustifiably so, and Robin immediately regretted it, lifting his hands, palms out. "Sorry, that was unfair." Jenn's wide eyes made him smile, but the multiple deaths, the reaper on Abigail's shoulder, the despair that had drained all color from his cousin's face, flattened the curve of his lips. "Take me to the bodies."

Liam led the way into the woods to where three bodies lay covered by blankets. Robin kneeled beside the smallest mound and pulled back the blanket. Olivia, his youngest cousin, in human form. The ground and leaves beneath her were dark from the blood that had seeped from the gunshot wounds to her chest and head.

Execution style.

He leaned closer, sniffed, then recoiled as silver stung his nostrils.

Beside her was another body, the shape of a coyote beneath the blanket. Pulling it back, he recognized Bruce by the dark patches of fur on his shoulders. His face, though . . . Robin had to look away. Bruce must have been mid-attack, protecting his cousin, when he'd taken a bullet to the face, the silver going clean through.

Robin glanced the few feet to the last coyote-shaped mound. His chest tightened with certainty, the evidence indisputable. Jenn's heightened distress, the reason she hadn't been with Pati and Pax, the uneasiness Robin had felt the closer he got to this place. It all made horrible, devastating sense.

He bowed his head, Jenn hiccupped a sob, and he had his confirmation. He didn't need to look under that third blanket. He stood instead and drew his cousin into his arms, holding her tight as they grieved for the man who'd been a father to both of them, to their pack. "I'm so sorry," he murmured into her hair.

"I should have—"

"You are the pack leader," Robin told her. "You did exactly what you're supposed to do. Jasper knew that. They all did."

He held his cousin while she sobbed, while he struggled to get his own emotions under control. His heart ached for his pack, for his uncle and cousins who'd been slaughtered. Ached worse for Jenn, understanding all too well the depth of her grief and the weight of the survivor's guilt bearing down on her. Crushing. His gut burned with rage at the person who'd injured his family, at Jasper for not taking more backup, at himself for leaving things the way he had, at Nature and Chaos for this whole fucked-up situation. Blood churned in his veins, urging him to run, urging him to exact mighty vengeance on all the people who'd done this to him and his.

More than anything, though, his soul longed for the one person who could settle the storm inside him.

He closed his eyes and recalled Atlas sitting across from him earlier in the night, the contemplative set of his elegant features, the weight of Altas's foot against his, the spring of his gaze and scent.

The acceptance and understanding that grounded Robin.

He inhaled deep and felt his soul settle, the instinct to run stayed for a little while.

He waited for his cousin to likewise settle, for her sobs to fade to sniffles, before he drew back. It wasn't nearly enough time for them to grieve the way they should, but they were up against a ticking clock none of them could afford to ignore. Pati and her son, the key to ending this awful game that kept taking from them, were missing.

"Did anyone hear the gunshots?" Robin asked.

"Nothing," Jason said. "And I would've been the closest."

Silver, plus a silencer.

The killer—or killers—weren't taking any chances. They'd covered their tracks too, no sign of footprints in the mud. But there were other signs and smells a tracker of average skill could follow. Bent tree limbs, broken stalks of winter weeds, bad coffee. Handing a steadier Jenn to

Abigail, Robin followed the trail to the service road that snaked through the property. Tire tracks in gravel gave some direction. "They went south," he told the others once they joined him. "Likely a van, given the size and spacing of the tracks."

"We think we know where they're headed," Abigail said, as Jenn dug something out of her pocket.

"We found these in Olivia's room." She dropped two game chips into his palm, branded with the name and logo of Dyami's casino in Nipomo.

Fuck, Atlas had been right; there'd been a traitor in the pack. He should have argued harder to keep Pati and Pax out of their lands, but where else could they go and still get the rest of the team there in short order? Still wasn't close enough.

He checked the time on his phone. "The kidnappers can't have made it to Nipomo yet."

"Mac was already here," Jenn said. "Came to the same conclusion. He's on the horn with other departments. They're putting up roadblocks."

"What did the van that took Atlas look like?" Abigail asked.

"Mangled metal, when I was done with it," Robin replied, but he followed her train of thought. Maybe there were more like it connected to Dyami's business or the people he employed, though Robin doubted this was the work of hired muscle like the goons who'd come after Atlas.

He doubted this was Dyami's work at all. It wasn't Evan's either. Not flashy enough, and by now, Robin would recognize Atlas's twin's scent, would never forget it. There was no trace of Evan on the air.

Nevertheless, the casino chips were the best lead they had. They dialed in Mac, Robin described the van, then also told them about Lucy. Atlas had been convinced she and her husband were forced to cooperate the last time. Lucy believed in Nature's cause, according Atlas. She believed in Pati and Pax. Perhaps she'd cooperate by choice with the other side.

All that said, even if this was Dyami, the casino seemed too obvious. They'd head to familiar territory, but not there exactly. "If they're smart, they'll stay off the main roads," Robin said.

Jenn clutched his biceps, giving his arm a squeeze. "That's why we need our best tracker on this."

THIRTY-ONE

It was midday before they found the van halfway down a ravine below the winding road from Pajaro to Matsun, the feline shifter from Club Sutro hanging dead in the front seat, pinned there not by the seat belt but by a crossbow bolt to the chest.

The occasional siren sounded from the elevated road overhead, the local sheriff's department having blocked it off a mile in either direction, but down here, it was just Robin and Mac and a hovering guard of ravens, the terrain too steep for humans.

Unless you were a warlock who could snap into the perfect position. Except Atlas's aim was off this time, his right foot landing on a clump of muddy soil that gave way under his heel. Robin tensed, ready to pounce, anything to stop Atlas from tumbling into the raging water below, but then Mac squawked an order and Robin's coyote obeyed on instinct, freezing in place.

Another snap later, Atlas reappeared a couple inches

over on a more stable incline. "Thanks for the assist," he said to Mac before turning his cocky smirk on Robin.

Who was sorely tempted to pounce for an entirely different reason. While they'd exchanged texts over the past eighteen hours, Robin hadn't heard his mate's voice or seen him in the flesh since the Canyon Lands. When Robin had left him to face down a deadly, determined witch alone. To kill her, as his texts had flatly informed the team. He'd survived whatever skirmish had resulted in Karoline's death, and now there he was, uninjured as far as Robin could tell.

Safe, relatively.

Like they needed to make Pax and Pati. The reasons they were there on the side of a mud-slick cliff, poking around an upside-down vehicle.

Atlas carefully bent to peer through the busted-out front windshield. "That's definitely Cyrus's handiwork." He narrowed his eyes, head tilted. "Is that the cat from the club the other night?"

Robin nodded. In retrospect, seeing how methodically and brutally the shifter had dispatched his uncle and cousins, how he'd risked handling silver to do it, Robin regretted putting Jason in his crosshairs at the club. If he'd gotten one of Mary's phoenixes killed . . . But it seemed the shifter hadn't realized who or what Jason was. Didn't matter now.

"Did you confirm Pati and Pax were in the van?"

Very carefully, Robin crossed in front of Atlas. Offering his hackles for balance and because he desperately needed the contact, Robin led him to the open back doors of the van. Inside was a baby bottle and Pax's blanket, one of the quilted ones Mac's mother had made.

Atlas conjured an orb and sent it slowly floating around the interior of the van. "No seats, no straps, nothing to hold on to," he said, cataloguing the same observations he and Mac had made. "If they'd been in there when the van went over the rail, there'd be blood, hair . . . bodies. No one could survive that."

The same conclusions too, especially given the one other piece of evidence Robin had to show him. They continued to carefully make their way to the driver's side where Robin stuck his muzzle through the open window and pointed it down, the direction of the pedals.

To where a cinder block was wedged against the gas pedal.

Atlas took one look through the window and whistled low. "Well, I guess that answers that question."

He didn't waste time on the precarious footing, letting Robin guide him back to a relatively stable ledge of rock. He leaned back against the wall of dirt, and Robin leaned against his front, keeping him secure and taking the contact he needed.

Atlas allowed it, indulged him more by combing his fingers through his fur as he talked through the evidence. "So, Dyami puts the feline hunter and your cousin in touch. She gets word to him that they're moving Pati and Pax, and he intercepts them." Robin appreciated the detachment in Atlas's summary and the acknowledgement of loss in his actions, a slow stroke over Robin's head, a lingering moment of silence, before he picked the debrief back up. "The cat wasn't actually headed for Nipomo." Robin swung his head around, ear cocked back at this new bit of intel. "Dyami is a silent partner in another casino in Matsun."

Matsun was halfway between YB and Nipomo. Close

enough to both paranormal and human populations, far enough from the dangers of YB but still close enough to get in on the action while still drawing the more adventurous, rebellious humans from the South. "The shifter took the coastal road, occasionally detouring through the forests, towns, and missions to hide his trail, before cutting back through these mountains to the interior, on the way to Matsun, when Cyrus intercepted him."

Robin barked in the direction of the last rest stop.

Atlas nodded. "That makes sense. He takes Pati and Pax at the rest stop, then takes out the cat and sets up this whole scene," he said with a wave of his hand at the upside-down vehicle. "First things first, Mac, can you get the cat's phone?"

The raven carefully glided inside the cab, then back out a moment later, device in his talons. He dropped it into Atlas's hand, and after a quick flick of the warlock's green magic over the screen, the phone was unlocked. Atlas's fingers flew over the screen, typing out something. Robin put his muzzle on the inside of Atlas's elbow, tugging the arm down so he could see.

"We're going to let Dyami know the package was intercepted," Atlas said, "By Robin. See if we can draw my brother out, once and for all." That done, he tucked the stolen phone away and glanced back the direction of the rest stop. "As for Pati and Pax, Cyrus either subdued them at the rest stop. Or . . ."

Mac's ominous croak put sound to the tingle of unease working its way up Robin's spine.

"*Or*, Pati left with him voluntarily."

Because she was afraid not to, Robin wondered, or a

more concerning possibility, no doubt the cause of his and Mac's unease, because Pati had been working with Cyrus all along.

THIRTY-TWO

Finding Cyrus took the rest of the day and the better part of the night. And the only reason they'd found him was because Paris had stepped in and called Lila's soul to him.

Mac had nearly had a coronary over the idea, which had been his husband's. After a day and night of police and tracking work turned up nothing, Paris had offered an alternative. If Cyrus had gone to his mother's house last time, was there another place that held meaning to them? And would Lila tell them? Mac had delivered enough evil souls to be extinguished, including Paris's own father, that he'd refused to believe Atlas when the warlock had assured them that the Lila who Paris might reach would be different, that it had been Chaos who'd infected her soul.

Mac wouldn't hear it, refusing to put his soulmate at risk. Robin couldn't say that if it was Atlas offering to do the same, that he wouldn't put up as fierce a fight. Atlas, of course, would tell him to fuck right off, and Paris was, lest anyone forget, Atlas's pupil. His delivery, though, was much gentler than Atlas's would have been, the medium reminding his husband that the clock was ticking. Solstice was two days away, and the future of peace was missing.

The raven had finally relented, but only with Liam, Mary, Jason, and Atlas on standby to channel the soul if it proved hostile. Unnecessary, it turned out; Atlas hadn't lied. Lila had only been doing what she thought was best for her son, what Atlas's father had encouraged her to do, what he made her. Based on the timing, Atlas had determined channeling Chaos into Lila had been the last spell his father ever cast before he'd turned to religion.

Nearly fifty years of Hail Marys to assuage his guilt.

Atlas had simmered with anger, the knowledge that his father was an even bigger asshole than he'd already thought rage-making, but he'd stashed the fury in a mental box somewhere and cooled down while Paris had finished painting the small coastal cottage Lila had shown him.

An hour later, Robin was hiding in the shadows of a cypress grove near said cottage with Atlas and Brock and Adam and Mac. "How do you want to handle this?" he asked Adam.

"Ambush," he replied. "Atlas snaps us all in together."

Atlas propped himself against the closest tree trunk. "You're assuming he doesn't already know we're out here."

"Can you put a shield around us?" Mac asked.

"As soon as we land, but not a second sooner, if we don't want to end up out there," he said with a jut of his chin toward the rough-and-tumble ocean, another storm moving in.

"Got it," Adam said. "That'll have to be soon enough."

"Smash and grab?" Brock asked.

"No," Robin said, and everyone's gaze shot to him. "He'll just keep coming. We're two days out. We can't afford another swerve like this. And if Pati's working with him—"

"She'll just try it again," Atlas finished.

"All right," Adam said. "Brock, you take perimeter. You two"—he gestured at him and Atlas—"neutralize Cyrus. Mac and I will talk to Pati." That division made sense: a warlock lookout, the two heavies on the threat, the inter-rogators on the unknown.

There was another variable Robin needed to know how to handle. "And if we have to kill Cyrus?" he said, gaze landing on Atlas. They'd both lost family to this war, so many, Robin most recently, and he was still tender, no time to grieve. And now Atlas's was in the crosshairs again. Recently discovered, and an enemy, but family, nonetheless.

Not a problem for Atlas. "Then we kill him."

Robin didn't buy it. "Atlas—"

"Don't," he said with a sharp shake of his head. "We share a sperm donor. That's it."

"But after we defeat Evan—"

"There will be only one Shaw left, assuming I survive."

Robin growled. That was not an outcome he would entertain.

"We need to go," Adam said. "Brock, you're up first."

The warlock snapped to the roof, landing silently, then after a moment, signaled them all clear. They positioned themselves so Adam, the human among them, was shielded, then, each with a hand on Atlas, rode his snap into the cabin.

And froze, the sight that greeted them catching them all off guard.

Pati was asleep on the couch beneath a colorful quilt, and in the rocking chair by the fire, under a similar quilt,

Cyrus sat cradling Pax against his chest. His other hand rested on his knee, gripping a pistol.

"No one fucking move," he said, voice as rough as his appearance, then with a flick of his brown gaze to Atlas, added, "And no spells either, brother."

"We're not here for you," Adam said, human to human.

"I know. You're here for Pati and this little eaglet." He gently patted the snoring baby's back.

"Do you know what you're holding?" Mac said, his voice calm and even. He had the skills of a trained investigator, combined with the empathy of a reaper. Made him a hell of a negotiator.

Usually.

Cyrus wasn't so easy a sell. "I know he's important. He has something to do with my mother's death." His gaze drifted back to Atlas. "At your mother's hands. I kill this baby, and my mother will be avenged."

"Or," Atlas said, "I can give you our father instead. A win for both of us."

Cyrus smirked, and for the first time, Robin saw the resemblance between brothers. There wasn't much else they shared in common—Atlas was a pretty pale package in a compact body; Cyrus was on the grizzled side of handsome, with dark hair and eyes and a scar that bisected his tan face, and a body that was almost too big for the rocker, Pax a small bean on his massive chest—but that twist of their lips, that shared arrogance was strikingly familiar.

Until Pax muttered a soft mewl, his little fingers curling in Cyrus's T-shirt, and the big man's smirk morphed into a soft, affectionate smile that Robin couldn't ever remember seeing on Atlas's face.

Mac saw it too. "You have no intention of harming that child, do you?"

"Of course not," Cyrus said. "He's innocent, just like his mother, like mine was too."

"Why have you been hunting Atlas?" Robin asked.

"Not just Atlas, all of them, so they couldn't do to another person what was done to my mother." His brown eyes glanced at Adam. "Your redhead saved me the trouble with the first one."

"The first one?" Atlas said, taking a step forward.

He would've taken another if Robin hadn't grabbed the back of his shirt, Cyrus's finger curling around the trigger, the truth he threatened to spill, sending twin bolts of fear through him. Now was not the time for another fucking swerve, and this one would send Atlas veering off the road. "He's baiting you," Robin said.

Atlas kept his foot on the gas. "You mean Canton? Brown hair, blue eyes, preppy clothes."

"That's the one. A few nights after he turned Icarus into a vampire and the girl with him into whatever she is."

Atlas moved again, but not forward. He dug his wallet out of his pocket and withdrew a folded photo. Two actually, another fluttering to the floor with the wallet Atlas tossed aside, too busy shoving the photo in his hand toward Cyrus. "This night?"

Robin ignored the photo on the floor, ignored his own safety, and moved between Atlas and his half brother. "He's got it wrong."

"Look at this picture." He practically shoved it in Robin's face. Canton was squared off with a snarling Icarus, Mary standing off to the side, the photo clearly taken from someplace close, a surveillance angle. Like Cyrus said, the job being done for him, but the picture failed to capture what happened next.

"Atlas, it wasn't him."

His eyes widened, a spark of yellow—betrayal—exploding in them. "You knew?" He lifted his other hand to snap, but Robin, well familiar with the action by now, stopped him short, shoving his fingers through Atlas's and threading them together. He held his mate to this awful reality, racing around the bend and off the road with him because he could no longer afford to lose him. None of them could. "She did it," he told Atlas. "So Icarus wouldn't have to."

Yellow spiraled through the green, and it fucking terrified Robin, made him fear he was about to lose Atlas to the other side, but his mate's hand gripping his back, holding on to him like a lifeline, meant Atlas was fighting to stay with him too. Robin kept hold of his hand while he lifted his other, gripping Atlas's face, keeping his focus solely on him, fighting together, just the two of them. "Think, Atlas. You would have done the same for Cole. And if that had been me, if you'd turned me into a vampire and Deborah into Nature, or vice versa, either of us would have killed to spare the other from doing so in that state. I love you, but I would have killed you for her."

Atlas's gaze held his while the green pushed back against the yellow, his better self responding to the logic. Robin fed it more. "Put it in the same box as your father. We'll deal with it later."

Another endless moment passed as the yellow faded. Atlas jerked his face free and cut a glare Adam's direction before he stepped over to the fire and threw the picture into the roaring flames.

"That's what she is, Nature?" Cyrus said, as Atlas leaned against the hearth. "And what was my mother?"

"Chaos."

He lifted his hand off Pax's back and gestured around the room. "Does this look like Chaos?"

"No, it looks and feels like peace." Everyone's attention swung the direction of the couch to where Pati was now sitting up, awake. She didn't seem fearful, just cautious as she took in the brewing conflict around her. Getting to her feet, she wrapped her blanket around her shoulders and stepped next to Cyrus's chair, her fingers softly combing over her baby's dark hair. "Which is what my son is."

"He's too young," Cyrus said, glancing up at her. "For any of this."

"Which is why we have to protect them," Mac said in his even negotiator tone from earlier.

Cyrus chuffed. "Fat lot of good you all have done with that."

"So you give it a try," Robin said, calling an audible. "If Pati is good with that?" At her nod, he explained his reasoning to the rest of the group. "His identity is scrubbed, he's a ghost, and no one knows about this place."

"Then how'd you find it?" Cyrus asked.

"Your mother told us," Atlas replied.

Cyrus was on his feet the next second, grizzled mug snarling at Atlas, the baby in his arms waking at the tension and letting out a wail.

Mac stepped between them. "Lila is good," he said, somehow keeping that calm tone even as the situation deteriorated around them. "My husband is a medium. He spoke to her. After she told us about this place, my brother, our reaper, delivered her."

"To?"

"Peace."

The tension left Cyrus's body, and he leaned into Pati beside them, their hands together on Pax's back. There was a connection there already. "Did you two know each other, before today?" Robin asked.

"No," Pati said, shaking her head. "But I knew right away that we could trust him."

Shared experience, years apart, but both part of this world not by their choice but by fate, who had seen fit to put them together.

Adam had come to the same conclusion. "We have a guard on the roof. We'll leave him here until we can get more of the pack in the area around you."

Cyrus opened his mouth to no doubt protest, and Robin beat him to it. "Not enough to give away your location and they won't bother you. Just backup, if you need it."

Cyrus looked to Pati, and at her nod, acquiesced.

"Good," Atlas said as he pushed off the hearth. "Since we're done here . . ."

Robin was too far away this time to stop him from snapping away. "Shit." He whipped his head to Adam. "Warn them."

He lifted his phone, text thread with Icarus open onscreen. "Already done."

"We need to get back—" He lost his words as his gaze caught on the other picture still on the floor. Golden eyes he'd only ever seen in pictures stared up at him, his mother's smiling face between two other blond women who were also smiling, their green eyes dancing. One was a mirror image of Daphne, only older, and the other . . . Now he knew where Atlas got his ethereal looks from—his mother. Who, along with Daphne's mother, clearly knew his. And Atlas knew this too? Had a picture of the three of them together in his wallet?

Betrayal found a new home, burning in Robin's gut as his head spun with the implications.

"Robin."

"What?" he barked at Mac and that even fucking tone, unhappy to be on the receiving end of it. Calm was the antithesis of everything swirling inside him.

"He bit," Mac said, holding the feline shifter's phone out to him.

"Who? Dyami?"

"No, Evan."

Robin glanced down at the screen, at the text thread open on it. The message Atlas had shot off to Dyami yesterday and a new reply. **Sunrise, Matsun casino. E will be there.**

THIRTY-THREE

On first glance, Evan looked almost exactly like Atlas. His blond hair was maybe a shade darker, there was a mole beside one eye that Atlas didn't have, and their eye color was different now, but otherwise they shared the same pale skin and elegant features. The same defiant set of their chins. And Evan was dressed in the sort of tailored suit Robin used to think Atlas preferred.

He sounded just like his twin too, haughty and smug. "So, you're my brother's mate?"

This was a mind fuck. Same as it had been earlier that month at the vineyard. Maybe even more so. That day, things had been moving a mile a minute—Daphne dead, an innocent to rescue, brothers hurling orbs at each other, and Nature hiding in the cottage up the hill. Today, it was just him and Evan in a dimly lit casino bar.

With time to consider and his coyote banked, Robin understood how, for the past ten years, they'd been chasing the wrong man. And now that he knew the real Atlas, knew him down to his scent, he also better understood how hard the performance must have been, how much of it he'd shouldered alone.

Never again.

"I am," Robin said, as he claimed the stool on the other side of the bar from Evan, who was pouring high-dollar whiskey into crystal tumblers.

"Has he told you that I was supposed to be your sister's?"

Robin clenched his jaw to keep it from hitting the bar.

Evan laughed and pushed a tumbler in front of him. "My dear brother, always keeping secrets. She picked not one but two other people over me."

The head spinning from back at Cyrus's cabin returned, but Evan's bitterness over Deborah focused the anger on the twin who well and truly deserved it. "Sore loser much?"

"I was for a while, and then I killed her."

The Robin of two months ago would have leapt across the bar. But this Robin recognized the bait for what it was. And this Robin had a mate—a lying one, albeit—he had to get back to. For the truth, about more than one thing. And because they had to work together if they were going to defeat the lookalike on the other side of the bar.

Robin tossed back the high-dollar bourbon like the low-class dog he was sure the slowly sipping warlock assumed he was.

Evan turned up his pretty nose and propped himself against the backbar. "Is he too much for you? Or not enough, like I clearly wasn't for Deborah? Is that why you're betraying him now?"

Robin laughed. "He's just right, actually." Atlas was smart, intense, arrogant, elegant, and filthy. He was wild at times, measured at others, and he was the only person in

Robin's life since Deborah who had made him feel settled. He reached over the bar for the whiskey, refilled his glass, then took a long drink before mentally asking Atlas for forgiveness as he borrowed his words for a lie he needed to tell. "But I don't do we."

Evan stayed leaned against the backbar, arms crossed, cut crystal tumbler against his lips. "Tell me more."

"I don't want a mate, I don't want a team, and I lost my family the day my sister died."

"You're a lone wolf."

"There's something inside here"—he tapped at his chest with the glass—"that makes me want to run. I want to be free. I don't want anything or anyone tying me down. I want to follow the jobs wherever they take me." The words that had come naturally before now tasted awful in his mouth.

But they did the trick, Evan polishing off his whiskey and setting his glass aside. "Your track record is impressive. Chaos could use you."

"One-time deal," Robin said with a sharp shake of his head. "You want Pati and her son, I can deliver."

"And your fee?"

He grabbed a napkin off the nearby stack, a pen from the cup by the register, and jotted down a figure and account number. He slid it across the bar to Evan.

The warlock balled it up and tossed it in the trash. "The money will be in your account when you deliver."

Robin threw back the rest of his drink, grabbed the bottle of whiskey, and slid off his stool. "No deal. Not how it works."

"How do I know you'll deliver?" Evan asked his retreating backside.

Robin spun on his heel mid-room. "You were the one who just commented on my track record." He tipped the bottle up for a healthy swallow, then wiped his lips off with the back of his hand. "Do you think I took payment afterward from any of them?"

"You drive a hard bargain, Mr. Whelan." He drew out his phone, tapped the screen a few times, and a moment later, Robin's phone vibrated in his pocket. Wire received. Evan grabbed another napkin, scribbled something on it, then strolled out from behind the bar.

Robin had another flash of cognitive dissonance, thinking he was seeing his mate approach in another damn suit. But as quick as the confusion came, it vanished with a single inhaled breath. All he could smell was the rotting stench of dark warlock, not a hint of spring.

Evan drew even with him and handed him the napkin. "Bring them there. Tomorrow night at eleven."

Robin pocketed the coordinates for the altar site in the Canyon Lands. The single weak spot in the veil, other than in La Purisima, that their team didn't control. "What are you going to do with them?"

"Use them to open the veil for Chaos to rejoin us."

Use them as sacrifice, more precisely. Robin forced his coyote not to snarl. Tough doing when Evan stepped closer. "Are you sure I can't tempt you?" He laid a hand on his chest and stared up at him with hooded yellow eyes. "One twin for the other. Maybe it was the two of us who were meant to be together."

As attracted as Robin was to Atlas, as he'd always been, he felt zero desire for the lookalike in front of him. Only hatred that he was certain would never turn into anything more. Not because he was fated to be with Atlas, but because the man in front of him was pure evil.

"Maybe our mothers got it wrong," Evan said, as he glided his hand higher.

Robin grabbed his wrist and yanked his hand off him. Not wanting his touch or the distraction. "Our mothers?"

"Ask my brother after you fuck him one last time." Evan's sly smile made the urge to strangle him harder and harder to resist. Made stealing the bottle back from his hand too easy, Evan turning on his heel and tipping the bottle up as he'd done. "Good day, Mr. Whelan."

Robin's head spun all the way to the parking lot, distracting him such that he missed the fact his car doors were unlocked. But he didn't miss the smell of intruder. He whipped around in the seat, prepared to strike, but Dyami slowly straightened with his hands raised, his palms outs.

"I'm here to help!" the pretender said.

"Since when?"

"Since I realized I was wrong." He handed Robin a folded piece of paper. "The real altar is here. Just call, and my people will be there. For peace."

THIRTY-FOUR

Robin didn't think twice about walking into Atlas's glitzy Sunset Hill high-rise. Evan had all but told him to go confront Atlas, to fuck him one last time. Robin intended to do both, and he hoped like hell it wasn't the last time for either.

He opened the door to Atlas's unit, wondering which would come first—fight or fuck. Finding Atlas in front of the floor-to-ceiling windows in nothing but a towel, water still dripping from the ends of his hair seemed to indicate a fuck was up first.

Until Atlas spoke and his voice was ice cold. "You lied to me."

Fight, then. "So did you."

Robin tossed his phone, wallet, and keys on the kitchen island where his mother's letters lay open and scattered. He'd left them at the condo when they'd swung by the other day. For safekeeping and for Atlas to read, hoping he might connect more dots for Robin. Seeing them strewn from one end of the island to the other made him regret the ask, brought his own anger back to simmering. He withdrew the photo of Willow and the Shaw women from his pocket and crossed the living room to Atlas. "Explain this to me," he barked, shoving the picture in Atlas's line of sight.

Atlas glanced at the photo, then back to the ocean outside his tinted windows. "You first."

The asshole still wouldn't give him anything.

Fine, he'd put his cards on the table first if it meant getting to the truths he wanted sooner. "For what it's worth, I didn't know Canton was your brother until that day in the vineyard. I don't think Mary or Icarus had made the connection until then either."

"Nature doesn't always tell her everything."

"Well, as soon as I found out, I tried telling you what happened, that day and on that rooftop in La Purisima."

Atlas whipped his gaze to him, and Robin was relieved to see his irises were green, the deep mossy shade he loved, no hint of yellow. "You couldn't just tell me?"

"Would it have made a difference?" he bit back, then regretted the tone when Atlas retreated, turning his gaze back to the waves. Robin tempered his tone and added, "I didn't mean to betray you."

"They were best friends," Atlas replied.

"Who?" Robin asked, the non sequitur catching him off guard.

He nodded at the photo in Robin's hand. "My mother, your mother, and Daphne's."

Except he'd never seen the other two women in that picture. Not in the flesh and not in any photo albums at the homestead. "If they were best friends, why weren't they around after Mom died?"

"Jasper forbade it." More dots connected: his uncle's distrust of outsiders, his skepticism of witches, his reluctance to travel any farther south than YB. "They kept their distance, and then they died."

"Casting Chaos out of Lila and behind the veil?"

Atlas nodded. "It's why Canton had to be the one to channel Nature into Mary. Mom and Vanessa, Daphne's mom, couldn't know who the new vessel was, in case they lost control of the spell and Lila got the information out of them."

"And where were you?"

"Keeping Evan distracted. He was keen to use the disturbance as cover for killing the woman who'd spurned him."

"Deborah."

"I stopped him that night. I couldn't that day. I'm sorry."

Robin turned from the view of the endless horizon, too much when his world was already starting to spin, and sank onto the living room couch. It was boringly modern and not particularly comfortable but it was squarely within the walls of the condo. "He said you were meant for me, and Deborah was meant for him. That our mothers had made it that way."

Atlas leaned back his head and groaned, not the good kind.

"Make it make sense, Atlas. Neither Deb nor I could understand what Mom was trying to tell us in those letters, other than vague notions of mates and Nature, and Jasper wouldn't say a damn thing either. He took whatever he knew to the grave with him. Same as Daphne. I need you to explain it to me. Please."

Atlas turned from the windows but rather than sit on the cushion beside him, he sat on the couch arm facing the bar. "Look at the colors of the ribbons. With everything you know now, *look*."

Green and yellow.

Green and yellow.

Robin gasped, dots connecting.

"They weren't just best friends," Atlas continued. "My mom, Sybil, and Vanessa worshiped yours. They were her disciples. Willow was the last time Nature and Chaos were joined in one vessel."

Robin had never been in a tornado, but he figured this mental and emotional whirlwind was what it felt like. "How?"

"Sheer force of will. They're not supposed to exist in one person, not until the eagle brings peace, but your mother held them as long as she could, until she ultimately succumbed to the most natural and chaotic thing on this earth, childbirth."

"She knew she wouldn't make it." That was why she'd written those letters—the uncertainty of what would happen to her and the magic inside her when she brought Deb and him into this world. And if his father had been anything like him, the guilt would have eaten him alive. Driven him to make it stop so he could be reunited with the love of his life.

Which left Deb and him.

"What happened to the magic? When Deb and I were born?" He swallowed hard and inhaled deep, the memory of wild mustard tickling his senses. "When Mom died?"

Atlas laid a hand on his shoulder. "When she died, my mom and Vanessa channeled the deities into new vessels.

But some of the magic was passed on to you and Deborah."

More and more dots connected.

His mother's written words about *wild* being only one of their instincts. Her coaching on how to use the magic inside them to silence that wild. Her lessons in tracking, in tending the homestead gardens, in using everything nature had to offer, that he and Deb would be uniquely able to detect and manipulate.

"She says in one of those letters that our mates would find us when Nature needed us most. Deb thought that was David and Adam. I thought I'd run from mine, forever."

"And I thought you two were intended to ground us, a twin for a twin, if Evan and I ever had to hold the deities. There were two of us, so it would be easier to share the load, to balance the forces and keep the peace until the eagle arrived. Until we had lasting peace."

"But that doesn't work anymore," Robin said, shaking his head. "Deborah is gone and Evan's evil. I looked the devil in the face today, and we can't let him have Chaos or Nature. Nothing good will come of it, and Pax is still too young."

"I know, and until tonight, I thought it was me who would have to hold them both instead. After all, it's what my mother named me."

"Balance."

"I was wrong."

Robin jerked his gaze to his; he hadn't seen the swerve coming. He parsed back through Atlas's words, through his mother's.

Until tonight.

Wild.

Magic.

Peace.

Balance.

More connections, the pieces coming together in a different way to form a new picture that caused Robin's chest to tighten and panic to swirl in his gut.

"No, no, no," he muttered. "Deborah was the good one. She was Nature. You don't want to give me Chaos either."

Atlas stretched out a hand, cupping Robin's cheek. "Don't think so little of yourself."

"But she was good."

"You are too. You both were, and the both of you were a little wild too, a little fearless, a little chaotic."

Robin huffed. "A little?"

"I was trying to be kind," Atlas said with a roll of his eyes that was both obnoxious and comforting. But then his face turned serious again as he pushed off the arm of the couch and came around to sit on the coffee table in front of him. "You both were primed, with a little bit of Nature and a little bit of Chaos."

"But Deborah's gone."

Atlas averted his gaze, guilt so obvious and familiar that Robin cursed himself for not recognizing it, for not making another horrifying connection sooner.

For not realizing that Atlas's high-end vodka was the same brand that was anonymously sent to him at the bar halfway around the world where he was drinking the night before Deborah's last pack call came in. When Robin had gotten so shit-faced he'd missed it. He'd blocked out everything from that night except the guilt from the consequences of his actions. But someone had helped him along.

"Are you the reason I didn't answer Deborah's call that day?"

Atlas righted his gaze and lifted his chin. "Yes."

Robin shot off the couch, nearly knocking Atlas off the arm in the process, all that simmering anger coming to a boil. "And to think, I came in here tonight thinking I'd told the bigger lie. First my mother"—he flung his arms wide, letting all the chaos hang out—"and now this!"

Atlas wasn't afraid of it, of him, in the least. He stepped directly in front of him and grasped his face. "This battle couldn't afford to lose you both. *I* couldn't afford to lose you, and I wasn't even in love with you then."

Robin's eyes grew wide, hearing those words out of Atlas's mouth.

And in the next breath, realizing he'd already said them to Atlas, earlier at Cyrus's cabin when it had been the warlock dangerously on edge.

Balance.

A fucking mirror, in more ways that Robin discovered every day.

The two of them, in this together.

"My brother was on the warpath that day," Atlas said. "He was twice jilted, and Vincent gave him the perfect cover. He wanted revenge and Chaos's attention, and he got both. By killing the woman who'd scorned him and who was also one of Nature's vessels. I wasn't going to let him have the other one. I made sure you were safe, and then I got to the scene as fast as I could, but I couldn't stop him. I tried, Robin. I promise you I tried with everything I had, but I wasn't strong enough, then."

His anger deflated as the overwhelming despair rushed

back in. "What am I supposed to do with this, Atlas? Any of it, all of it?"

Atlas eased the grip on his face, gently holding his cheek as he closed the distance between them. "It was supposed to be the two of you, a shared burden, but now you have to be the strong one."

Too much, too wide, more than the peaks and valleys of the range that stretched around their homestead. He shook his head, eyes slipping closed, breaths coming short as he faltered. "That's not me, Atlas. I'm a traitor."

Atlas cupped the other side of his face and pressed their foreheads together, making Robin's world smaller, making it so he could breathe. "You made a mistake that I helped you make. That doesn't make you a traitor."

"But Paris—"

"Was not a mistake, and the team has forgiven you. They'll rally behind you."

"Atlas, I run, *that's* who I am." He'd thought he'd changed when he'd stood in that casino bar with Evan, but that was before the rug had been yanked out from under him. Before his old world had been turned upside down by back-to-back revelations that put the weight of said world on his shoulders. He was not the man for that job. Deborah could have done it, but not—

Atlas's lips brushed over his, silencing the whirlwind. Settling him. "If you run, I will run with you. I will run with you forever." He drew back far enough for Robin to see the truth in his dark green gaze. "But you can't run from your soul, Robin. And neither can I."

He held his stare another long moment, his whole world right in front of him, his mate. The world didn't seem so scary, so big in the forest. In the eyes of the man magic had put in his path but who had found his own way into Robin's heart. "You settle me," he told him.

"And you balance me," Atlas replied, thumb skating over his cheek.

Robin would do anything to keep that, to keep him, including the thing that scared him the most. He inhaled deep and nodded. "All right," he said. "We face it. We fight."

A smirk turned up one corner of Atlas's lips. He lowered a hand and loosened the knot in the towel at his hip, the damp terrycloth hitting the floor. "After we fuck."

And because Atlas hadn't given him anything earlier, Robin resisted giving him the easy win now. One last fight, since they did it so well. "I don't answer to you."

Atlas's eyes sparkled, spring in all the shades of green. "But my soul answers to yours."

Robin brought their lips back together, bruising and soft. Balanced. "And mine to yours."

The only fight after that was over where to fuck: against the windows—too distracting; on the couch—too soft; in the bedroom—way too far away. They settled on the living room floor, with Atlas astride his lap, riding his cock, while Robin stroked Atlas's length with his spit-slick fist. Getting them off together just as the fog rolled back from the shore, giving way to the bright midday sun that streamed in through the windows and painted a sweaty head-thrown-back Atlas in shades of orange and gold.

On fire, with no shield between them to stop the smell of spring from filling the air around them, from filling their souls.

Robin would fight anyone to protect this connection, this mate he'd never wanted and now couldn't imagine his life without. And when it was all over, he couldn't wait to run with Atlas out there in the sun.

THIRTY-FIVE

"Evan wants us to think tomorrow night's spell will take place at the altar in the Canyon Lands." Robin rested his forearms against the back of the chair at the head of the cellar tasting table, next to where Atlas sat, as far away from Mary and Icarus at the other end as possible. The warlock might understand why Mary had killed his older brother, but he wasn't ready to forgive her yet. Robin couldn't blame him.

"Where's it going down for real?" Jason asked from Atlas's other side.

"La Purisima."

Icarus dropped the sweater he was panic crocheting, the metal hooks clattering to the table, his forehead following suit as he thunked it against the weathered wood. "Fuck me."

"Home sweet home," Atlas singsonged, and Robin bit the inside of his cheek, fighting a grin. It was a cheap shot, but Atlas's haughty poking at Icarus felt like the most normal thing in the world right then.

"But LP is full of humans," Paris said, dampening the admittedly ill-timed humor. The medium was no doubt already contemplating the cleanup work, assuming they survived. He, Mac, and Liam would be busy for days.

"Like picking sacrifices off a tree," Adam correctly assessed.

"It's risky," Abigail said. "The humans could turn on them."

"Or on us," Robin added.

"What happens when you don't show up with Pati and Pax?" Jenn asked from Robin's other side.

"We'll call Evan and tell him I killed them." Robin took the stack of printouts Atlas handed him and tossed them onto the table. Photos of a staged massacre. "I'll tell Evan what he thinks he already knows. That I'm a traitor."

"Why would Evan believe you?" Adam asked.

"Because Deborah betrayed him already," Atlas said. "She was supposed to be his mate, and she chose David and you over him."

A wide-eyed Adam propped his elbows on the table and held his head in his hands. Robin felt for his friend. Been there, done that, got the head spinning. Icarus coasted a hand over his shoulder while Mac picked up the interrogation.

"He'll have a backup plan," the raven said to Atlas. "It won't be as powerful as Pati and Pax would've been, but he'll be ready."

"Good thing we have the last barrier between him and Chaos."

Gazes drifted toward Mary until Robin straightened. "Not her, me."

Icarus whipped his head up, ginger brows racing north. "You?"

"Evan wants Chaos. I'm ready to take them both. Like my mother did. Like Deborah and I were supposed to do together."

Multiple gasps of "What?" echoed around the table, except from the green-haired pixie at the other end.

"I thought it was me and Evan," Atlas explained. "That we were supposed to hold Nature and Chaos together, with Robin and Deborah as our anchors, but Evan's unanchored and only interested in Chaos. If he succeeded in bringing Chaos through, I was going to channel them both into me and balance the ends, with Robin as my anchor, but it was never me." He glanced up at Robin, the confidence in his gaze making Robin stand that much taller. "I'm the anchor, he's the vessel."

Questions erupted.

"What's that mean?" from Jason.

"What's he have to do?" from Paris.

"Will he make it?" from Jenn, her voice rough as she turned in her chair toward Atlas. "I can't lose any more family."

"He'll make it," Atlas said, reaching across the chair between them and covering her hand. "If I have anything to say about it."

"The phoenixes are ready," Mary said. "The other warlocks and witches too."

All the work Atlas had been doing with her when he wasn't with him the past two weeks. "You're ready to let it go?" Robin asked her.

Mary's hazel gaze slid to Atlas. "As he's told me multiple times, I was only a vessel."

But she was family to the man beside her. "Will she survive it?" Icarus pressed.

"Will you kill me if she doesn't?" Atlas bit back, and Robin clenched his jaw. He could give Atlas the prior dig, but this one was a push too far, especially when emotions were raw and life as they knew it was on the line.

He prepared to step in, to defuse the situation, but Mary beat him to it. "It's my choice, Icarus. I'm ready to be the old lady who complains about her little brother and his rowdy friends. I'm ready to live my life." She shifted her gaze to him. "Are you ready to give up yours?"

"I'm not giving up anything," Robin said. "I'm taking responsibility." He split a glance between Jenn and Adam. "I'm doing for her what I should have done ten years ago. I'm here now. And I'll stay here until Pax is ready."

"You'll be a target," Mac said. "Even if you kill Evan, someone will always come for you."

"They'll have to go through me first." Atlas threaded their fingers together, and Robin couldn't help but smile. All the times he'd done the same to keep Atlas from snapping away, from running, and now Atlas was tying them together. No more running. "Can he count on all of you?"

Adam rose first, walking the length of the table to where Robin stood and throwing his arms around him. "She would be so proud of you. I'm here for you, whatever you need."

Paris shot out of his chair next and practically launched himself at Robin. "Thank you for giving him a chance," he whispered, and Robin grinned through the wet in his eyes. "I'm with you."

Mac was next, a hug as calm as his husband's had been enthusiastic. "I and the rest of the flock are behind you."

One by one, the others followed, a hug and a pledge, until only Jenn was left.

When his cousin moved to lower her head in deference, Robin gently clasped her shoulder, stopping her short. "Don't," he said. "You are the pack leader, and a damn good one. Better than I ever would've been." He lowered his head to her instead, but only for a moment before Jenn yanked him into a crushing hug.

"Your pack will be there for you," his leader said. "Always."

THIRTY-SIX

"Where are you?" Evan snapped in greeting.

"If you're referring to the traitor," Atlas replied into Robin's phone that he held between them, the two of them standing on the end of the lake dock, slightly away from their gathered forces. "He's in my favorite pair of silver handcuffs."

Robin liked the sound of that—well, not the silver part—but the mention of handcuffs in Atlas's confident, haughty tone was a welcome reprieve after twenty-four hours of nonstop apocalypse prep. He and Atlas hadn't even had time for an end-of-the-world fuck, and he was pretty damn sure Adam and Mac had each gotten that courtesy when it had been their turn in the shit.

"Looks like he betrayed you too," Atlas added, and Robin tuned back in. At his mate's nod, he pressed Send on the pictures Cyrus had staged. They watched as the delivery notification beneath the text bubble changed from Sending to Delivered to Read, then waited as the silence from the other end dragged on.

No words, no sound, no reply from the other warlock.

Atlas continued to needle, tsking his brother. "I thought you would've learned your lesson by now. First Deborah, now Robin. But I guess it wasn't so bad this time. The dog just took your money and ran, not your whole reason for existing."

A low menacing snarl rumbled over the line.

"I can give you a reason again," Atlas said, tone mimicking Mac's when he was negotiating, calm and even, offering Evan the redemption Robin had been sure he would. "There's still work to do, brother. Last offer."

Evan didn't take the out. "You're an idiot if you think I don't have a backup plan."

"I fully expect it," Atlas replied, infusing his voice with equal strength, two powerful warlocks squaring off. "You won't win this. And you won't see our mother on the other side. You won't keep your promise."

Another long pause, and then, "I broke it a long time ago. She won't be surprised," before the line went dead.

Decision made, fate sealed.

Robin ended the call and handed Atlas the phone. "What did you all promise her?"

"That we'd join her in peace when peace also existed on this side of the veil."

"You'd have to make all the right choices to get there." It was a heavy ask on its own, but that wasn't all Sybil had asked of her sons.

"It's not been easy." He tucked the device in his pocket, then looked up with unguarded eyes, the first time Robin had ever seen him so open. "You were the hardest one to make."

Robin was tempted to cup his cheek, to return soft with

soft, but that wasn't the balance Atlas needed, not right now. He gripped his face instead, rough, the way he needed it, and held him firm, green clashing with gold. "Thank you for making the right one."

He smashed their lips together, drowning in spring one last time before taking the dive into winter, hoping like hell they made it out the other side.

"Anytime now," Icarus snarked from the lakeshore behind them, popping the bubble around the small world he and Atlas had made for themselves on the end of the dock.

Robin didn't feel overwhelmed, though. Atlas had insisted they stage their forces here, on the lake where Robin had spent countless hours with his sister, where the range and world out there didn't feel so big. Atlas had done it for him, when he'd needed it most.

He squeezed the warlock's fingers, threaded through his own, as they returned to the shore.

"He said no?" Mary asked.

"Did you expect anything else?" Atlas replied.

"A deity can hope."

"The time for hope has passed," Adam said. "It's time for action."

"To end this," Robin agreed. "Word from recon?" he asked Mac.

"Site confirmed," he answered. "The revival field in La Purisima, like Dyami told us."

Icarus leaned his head back on a pained groaned. "Fucking irony."

His partner, however, was focused on logistics. "How many?" Adam pressed for details.

"So far, the flock reports a fieldful."

"And Evan?" Atlas asked.

"Not there yet, but the altar is ready."

For whomever he appeared there with, like he and the giant had appeared with Paris at the Stick. All the giants were gone now, though, so who would be at Evan's side tonight? Who would help him channel the souls to thin the veil? Who would be the sacrifice on the altar? Judging by the location of the moon, they were five minutes from finding out. "You're sure you can get us all there?" he asked Atlas.

The warlock glared at him through narrowed green eyes. "Fuck you for even asking."

Robin grinned; there was the Atlas he loved. "We're ready," he told Adam, and the call went down the line and through the crowd to move to their designated positions in the forest. A phoenix paired with a warlock or witch at each point of the star, the pack gathered around the arc between each point, the rest of their forces inside the circle. Adam and Icarus, Mac and Paris, and Liam, Jenn, and Abigail in a close circle around Atlas, Mary and him in the center of the giant forest pentagram.

Nature at its most powerful.

Robin barely got the "I love you" out before Mary and Paris shouted "Go," their sense of the thinning veil keener than the rest, and Atlas dropped to his knees, digging his hands in the dirt. Lines of green magic shot across the ground, bringing the pentagram to life, and Robin was powerless to resist the shift, same as every other shifter in the circle.

And when the phoenixes and magicians put their hands to the ground too, fire and magic racing back on either side of Atlas's green and colliding with Mary in the center, completing the circuit, it was as if the earth fell out from under Robin's paws.

THIRTY-SEVEN

He landed in a field, paws hitting hay, and as soon as he lifted his head, several things became clear.

While there were paranormals among the crowd they'd ported into, most of the people there were humans.

Said humans seemed to be there for a revival, led by the priest sitting shirtless on the altar of plywood and two-by-fours, railing about sin and the ultimate sacrifice to cleanse his soul. The same priest, Niall, who'd sinned with Atlas in a club earlier that month.

And behind the altar stood a sharp-dressed warlock holding a knife and on either side of him were two older men holding the priest's outstretched arms. One of the men shared the same blond hair and nose as Atlas's deceased cousin. The other wore a smirk that matched that of his son beside him . . . and of his other son, the man Robin loved.

Robin threw back his head and roared at the betrayal— of Atlas, of Sybil, of Deborah and his own mother.

Their presence announced, pandemonium erupted.

Some of the humans ran. Others revealed weapons

they'd hidden under their jackets. They'd been primed, by the priest and supposed converts behind the altar with Evan. Adam gave the call to spare them when they could, Jenn echoing it to the pack, but a crossbow was a crossbow, and as their group made their way forward in the crowd, Robin didn't hesitate to bite into any human aiming at his family. Same as Atlas beside him, hurling green orbs of magic, and Mary, slinging knives at anyone who got close to their fighters.

"Atlas!" Paris shouted from where he was crouched beside one of the dead. "The altar!"

Robin slung the latest attacker aside and rounded behind Atlas, stomach sinking at the sight a half crowd away. Long bloody slashes crisscrossed Niall's chest, and deep cuts bisected the insides of his arms, blood spilling out of him. Pierce and James moved to either end of the alter, Evan remaining in the middle, and the magic that rippled over the field was awful, like it was a wind scooping up souls and sending them skyward.

It chilled Robin's insides and made his stomach churn, the dreadful dark magic stench left behind only adding to the nausea.

"We need to get to that altar!" Atlas shouted.

Robin howled for backup, and Jenn and Abigail joined him in a point, more of the pack flanking them, clearing a path forward by claw and teeth, for Jason and Atlas who were likewise hurling orbs of fire and magic at anyone who got in their way.

Adam, Icarus, and Paris, with Mary between them, were also making their way forward, while Mac, Liam, Kai, and the rest of the ravens sailed higher, maneuvering above the altar, avoiding enemy orbs while trying to intercept the souls the evil warlocks were using like a battering ram against the veil.

"I thought you two were done with magic?" Atlas shouted at his father and uncle when they were close enough to be heard. They were still fighting their way through what appeared to be the other side's best fighters at the base of the altar, other shifters and warlocks tempted Chaos's promise of power.

"He's closing the veil once and for all," Pierce called back. "Like you and Daphne, and Sybil and Vanessa would never do."

"We're finishing this!" James added.

"Is that what you think he's doing?" Atlas scoffed.

"He's thinning it, you morons," Jason shouted. "He wants to bring Chaos through."

"He's ending this!" Pierce continued to insist, but James was wavering, his hold on the altar and the magic loosening.

Adam noticed the same. "Paris!" he shouted. "Call Daphne to you." The problem with thinning the veil was that it could work in their favor too. The souls being swept up coalesced around the stately blond who appeared a moment later over her father's shoulder. "Daddy, stop," Daphne said. "He's using you like he used me."

Paris didn't stop there. Canton and Cole appeared next, and Atlas gasped beside him.

"Dad, stop this!" Canton pleaded. "Don't make our deaths for nothing."

"Evan, if you stop now," Cole begged, "I'll forgive you, Mom will forgive you."

And then Lila, adoringly wrapping herself around Pierce. "Your sons need you."

"Argh!" Pierce shouted, letting go of the altar.

For a second, as Robin and his contingent broke through the line, he thought victory was within their grasp, but then Pierce whirled on his heel, set his sights on Paris, and spun up a globe, arm reared back.

Robin tensed to jump, to vault over the altar if that was what it would take to prevent Pierce from hurling that globe at the best of them. But he didn't need to. Green magic streaked past him and collided with Pierce, sending him tumbling.

Robin whipped around in time to see pain streak across Atlas's face, to feel it in his own chest. A kill his mate hadn't wanted to make but one he'd had to—to protect his real family.

And Robin acted to protect his. Sensing a threat to Atlas, he spun back around, just in time to see Evan cast a yellow globe in their direction. Robin flattened Atlas, taking Mary down with them, the tip of his other ear taking the singe.

And fuck if that didn't piss him off more.

End this! the wild called inside him.

"Get what you deserve," Mary whispered in his ear.

He roared for his pack, and they answered, rushing to meet him at the foot of the altar, jumping after him, as he leapt the altar, sending Evan wheeling backward.

The force of Adam's bullet, Atlas's green globe, and Robin's big coyote body all hitting him at once took him to the ground.

Robin stood on the laughing warlock's chest, Jenn on one arm, Abigail on the other, as blood leaked out of his wounds. But once Adam and Atlas joined them, Evan's laughter stopped and his words, gargled through blood bubbling on his lips, turned Robin's insides even to ice. "I never intended to live." His yellow eyes, swirling with gray, drifted overhead. "You brought Chaos through the veil. Not me." Nearly all gray, they traveled back to Atlas. "My backup plan, brother."

After one last gasp, his chest stilled under Robin's paws.

And then the earth heaved, worse than any jolt he'd felt in YB since the Rift, and he was knocked off balance.

A yawning canyon opened in the ground and swallowed the altar whole. Threatened to swallow more. "Robin!" Atlas shouted. "Help me!"

He rolled back onto his feet, just in time to get a paw around Mary before the canyon took her.

"Higher ground!" Adam shouted, and everyone who could got a hand on a warlock who snapped them to the ridge at the other end of the field. But their position wouldn't last long, the canyon growing wider with each shake of the earth.

Atlas landed crouched beside him and laid a hand on his chest. "Shift!" he ordered, and Robin's magic answered, putting him back in human form. "Are you ready?" Atlas asked him.

"Do it now." The future of his pack, the lives of his family, of his mate depended on it.

Atlas pressed a kiss to his lips. "I love you too."

It was the last thing Robin remembered before magic seared through him, Atlas's and the other witches' and warlocks', the burning life fire of the phoenixes, the souls that Paris called to him, the magic some of them brought to bear, including Sybil's and Vanessa's, Daphne's, Canton's, and Cole's.

Ripping him from one end to the other.

Magnets pushing against each other.

Like he would never be put back together again.

The terrifying distance between one piece of him and the other.

The span of every wide-open space that had ever made him feel claustrophobic.

Like he'd never be able to run far enough to put it all back together.

Blood pounding in his ears and racing through his veins.

His coyote crying out.

His mother's, his twin's answering.

His pack answering, coming together around him with the rest of his family, bounding him in and making it so he couldn't be ripped so far apart.

Making it like he was back on the dock in the forest.

A whisper of spring tickled his nose, and then warm lips brushed his forehead. "I'll run with you."

Mate.

His blood calmed, the magic settled, his soul—both sides of it—planted.

He opened his eyes and gasped. Atlas's green gaze was swirled through with another color. Not yellow, but gold. Like his. And reflected in them were his own, swirling with green.

He lifted a hand, gripping his face. "Mine."

Atlas gripped his face right back. "Mine."

Their lips connected, "yours" a promise they both made, forever.

THIRTY-EIGHT

Robin was beginning to think Mac's family should just leave the festival tent up year-round. It had gone up for Samhain, stayed up for Mac and Paris's wedding, and now was playing host to Yule.

All his family under one tent, sparkling lights strung from one side to the other, making reality seem like a fairy tale.

His pack, Jenn and Abigail and others from the homestead and nearby range, joining after the funerals today and camping here for the remainder of the holidays.

The extended family Deborah had brought into his life, Icarus on Adam's lap as they debated with Mac and Paris and Jason and Kai over how long it would take to reopen Club Sutro this time.

Even the family that had recently come with Atlas, Cyrus cradling a sleeping Pax while not being shy at all about his interest in a once-again fully human Mary, who was dancing up a storm with Pati.

Robin stood on the outskirts of it all, leaned against a sturdy tent pole, sipping a beer and, for the first time in his life, not feeling like an outsider.

He'd fought for them, and they'd fought for him too, answering his call and helping to hold him together when it had felt impossible.

They were his, and he was theirs.

But there was someone else he belonged to first.

He went searching for his mate, unsurprised to find him stretched out on a chaise under the pergola, smoking a joint and watching the sunset. "Trade you?" he said, offering the beer for a hit.

Atlas wrinkled his nose. "Not if that beer was the last beverage on earth."

"Because that sort of absolute worked out so well for you the last time."

Atlas handed him the joint and flipped him off in the same motion. Sexy fucking asshole.

Robin tossed the beer bottle aside, then lowered himself onto the side of his chaise, a hand on Atlas's stomach while he smoked. It had become a habit after LP, always needing to have a hand on Atlas when he was near. Maybe it would pass, eventually, but it helped him feel settled. And Atlas didn't seem to mind.

"You doing okay?" Atlas asked, a less pleasant habit he'd picked up after LP.

Careful to keep the joint off the furniture and his mate, he stretched over Atlas. "For the last fucking time, I'm good. Better than, even. And if I'm ever not, I will tell you."

Atlas held his gaze, seeming to assess the truth of his promise, and finding it sufficient, huffed out a "Fine."

Robin chuckled. "You're grumpy today."

"I'm not grumpy, I'm horny. We saved the world, and it's been nonstop festival or family ever since. We didn't even get to fuck before—"

Robin cut off his rant with a kiss that was admittedly more laughter than passion, but the direction of Atlas's thoughts had so closely mirrored his own that he couldn't help but find the humor in their mutual frustration. He snuck a hand under his kilt and fondled his bare balls.

"That's not nice," Atlas muttered against his lips. "On either count."

"Snap us to your vineyard."

Atlas drew back, meeting his gaze. "Why?"

"Because I want to roll around in the dirt with you. I want all this"—he trailed a finger along the underside of Atlas's stiffening cock—"in its natural element."

He'd barely finished the last word when he landed on his back between the rows of vines, Atlas tearing open his flannel and attacking his chest, tongue swirling around one then the other nipple before Atlas seemed to get lost in the divot between his pecs, like he'd nuzzle there all day and night given the option.

But Robin had other ideas, starting with ridding the warlock of his shirt. He pushed the tight black tee up and off, wanting to see the oranges and reds, the yellows and pinks of sunset painting his skin like they had that day on the dock. Wanting to taste every inch of the skin he hadn't gotten to enjoy that day. The soft spot behind Robin's ear, the sharp line of his clavicle, his nipples that shriveled on contact.

Atlas held him there by the back of his head. "Harder," he moaned, as he rocked in his lap. Robin was happy to oblige, sucking his nipple hard between his lips, then nipping it with his teeth. A quick, rough lash with his tongue, then repeating it all over. Making Atlas writhe in his lap, and with his kilt rucked up between them, the tip of his cock leaking against Robin's abs.

His own cock ached, trapped in his jeans while Atlas rutted bare against him, but he'd do this all night if it was what Atlas wanted, what he needed. Atlas had given him exactly that—what he needed. Peace, family, and a place for his soul to feel settled. Acceptance of and relief from the guilt that had plagued him for so long. He wanted to do and be the same for Atlas, always.

Warm lips tickled his ear. "You can fuck me now."

Given the green light, he'd happily step on the gas.

Tipping forward, he laid his mate in the dirt, flipped his kilt up, and wasted no time taking his cock to the back of his throat and swallowing around the tip. Atlas moaned, arching his back and digging his fingers into the soil, making the scent of it all even more potent. Making Robin hungrier than he'd ever been for his mate.

Atlas too, one hand curling in his hair, flecks of dirt tickling Robin's cheek as it rained down around him. "That wasn't a request. Get your cock in my ass. Now."

One more pass over his dick, then Robin drew back to ditch the rest of his clothes. Half propped up, Atlas spit in his palm to stroke over Robin's length to help get him ready, while Robin did the same with his hole, stretching it with spit-slick fingers the way Atlas liked.

Then stretching him with his cock, pushing in hard and fast, all the way to the hilt.

Atlas sighed, the tension fading as they settled into their rhythm. Robin planted his forearms in the dirt on either side of his head, fingers playing with the tips of his hair, nose buried behind his ear so he could smell Atlas and the earth, nature in one breath, while their lower bodies chaotically drove them toward their climax.

"Tomorrow morning," Atlas panted in his ear as they raced toward the end. "I want to run with you." He arched his body, one hand plowing through his hair, the other through the dirt. "In the sun."

Robin gasped against the side of his face. So close. "It's a date, mate."

Atlas's "ugh" died on a moan as he came, cock erupting between them, painting Robin's torso with come, the heat and the smell tripping Robin the rest of the way over too.

When he came back to earth, Atlas was smirking up at him, green and gold eyes dancing. "You should be ashamed of yourself for that line."

Robin nipped at his sexy grin. "How much do you hate me for it?"

"So much," Atlas groaned dramatically, then with a snap, flipped them over and threaded his fingers through Robin's, pressing their hands into the dirt and their foreheads together, Robin's whole world right there with him. "But I love you more."

Robin's lips curved against his. "Balance."

————

For all the latest updates on new projects, sneak peeks, and more, sign up for Layla's Newsletter and join the Layla's Lushes Reader Group on Facebook.

————

Reviews are an invaluable tool when it comes to spreading the word about great reads. Please consider leaving an honest review for *Atlas and the Traitor* on your favorite review site.

Thank you for reading!

ACKNOWLEDGMENTS

Yeah, so about all those coyotes I cursed… In truth, I was fascinated with them at first, especially during the pandemic when that shot of one on the Golden Gate Bridge was published. I think that was when the idea of Robin was born. He became an asshole once we moved to San Diego, into a house that backed up to a canyon, and we had to deal with the howling outside every night, all night. I was also determined to actually do an enemies-t0-lovers romance. Robin and Atlas were definitely my enemies as I wrote them, probably all that cursing I did, but eventually I loved them, and I hope you did too!

Helping me bring this story to life were Adam on copy edit and Lori on proofreading, Kelley with another stunning design created around the steamy photo of Kyle from Kevin D. Hoover, Kim on the beta read and PA support, Hailey and Annabeth on sprints that this book would not be done without, and Lushes for cheering this duo on. Thank you all!

ALSO BY LAYLA REYNE

For the most up-to-date list of titles and a helpful reading order, please visit www.laylareyne.com.

Soul to Find:

Icarus and the Devil

Jason and the Storm

Paris and the Reaper

Atlas and the Traitor

Agents Irish and Whiskey:

Single Malt

Cask Strength

Barrel Proof

Tequila Sunrise

Blended Whiskey

Angel's Share

Fog City:

Prince of Killers

King Slayer

A New Empire

Queen's Ransom

Silent Knight

What We May Be

Perfect Play:

Dead Draw

Bad Bishop

King Hunt

Best Play

Table for Two:

The Last Drop

Dine With Me

Blue Plate Special

Over a Barrel

Changing Lanes:

Relay

Medley

Freestyle

ABOUT THE AUTHOR

Layla Reyne is the author of *What We May Be* and the *Agents Irish and Whiskey*, *Fog City*, and *Perfect Play* series. She writes sexy, intense LGBTQIA+ romance featuring competent adults in kitchens, sports arenas, car chases, and other high-stakes situations. Whether it's adrenaline-fueled suspense, rival athletes, vampires and shifters in alt-realms, or love mixed with mouth-watering foodie goodness, queer folks finding happily-ever-afters is guaranteed.

You can find Layla at laylareyne.com, in her reader group on Facebook—Layla's Lushes, and at the following sites:

BB bookbub.com/authors/layla-reyne

facebook.com/laylareyne

instagram.com/laylareyne

tiktok.com/@laylareyne